Adeline Sergeant

An Open Foe

Vol. 1

Adeline Sergeant

An Open Foe
Vol. 1

ISBN/EAN: 9783337347086

Printed in Europe, USA, Canada, Australia, Japan

Cover: Foto ©Andreas Hilbeck / pixelio.de

More available books at **www.hansebooks.com**

AN OPEN FOE

A Romance

BY

ADELINE SERGEANT

AUTHOR OF 'BEYOND RECALL.'

' Who with repentance is not satisfied,
Is not of heaven nor of earth.'

IN THREE VOLUMES
VOLUME I.

LONDON

RICHARD BENTLEY & SON, NEW BURLINGTON ST.
Publishers in Ordinary to Her Majesty the Queen
1884

CONTENTS.

AN OPEN FOE.

PART I.—A TANGLED WEB.

CHAPTER I.

HUSBAND AND WIFE.

It was nine o'clock in the morning. The May sunshine fell in a perfect flood of radiance upon the eastern side of a small white house, situated upon a wide and breezy down which overlooked the sea. No other building was visible, although the town of Elmstone was barely two miles distant. The house—it was little more than a cottage—was sheltered from the winds, and to some extent concealed from the eye of a casual observer by a ridge of rising ground behind and a clump of fir-trees before it. There was a cheerful-looking little garden and pleasant

1

shrubbery; and the walls of the house were nearly hidden by creeping plants, green-leaved only as yet and not in blossom. The house nestled so snugly in this retired nook that one might well have fancied it to be the resting-place of some recluse who had grown weary of the world.

But no sign of weariness of the world would have been found in the occupants of that little white house on the fine May morning of which we write. On the contrary, both master and mistress were eager to quit this rural retreat and see a little more of the restless world from which their dwelling-place seemed so far away. They sat—master and mistress—at each end of the breakfast-table : the master, with a newspaper on his knees and a letter in his hand; the mistress toying with a fragment of toast upon her plate. Their little boy, a child of three years old, was playing with a favourite setter upon the hearth-rug. A fire burned in the grate, for the morning, though one of brilliant sunshine, was undeniably chilly. The child basked in the blaze and talked to the dog. His voice was the only one that had been heard for some minutes in the room, for the father and mother had been silent for the last quarter of an hour, and sat with averted eyes and faces on which the traces of care and vexation were sadly manifest.

It was the young man who at last looked up and broke the silence.

"Come, Lucy," he said, "don't be angry. You need not mind what people think. This state of things will not last long."

"But I do mind what people think!" she broke out passionately. "Do you suppose when I married you that I expected to keep our marriage a secret for full four years? I have risked everything for you; and you care for me so little that you will do nothing at all for me."

She pressed her handkerchief to her eyes and began to sob. Something in the very violence of her emotion seemed to grate upon her husband's ear. A keen observer might have said, indeed, that the momentary frown upon his forehead was caused by a certain lack of refinement and self-control, which made itself evident in the raised tones of her voice and the excitement of her manner. But Gaston Ravenscroft's frown very speedily faded, and was succeeded by a gentler look. He could never be long angry with her. In fact it was difficult for any one to be long angry with Lucy Ravenscroft, for she was a young woman with a striking and rather pathetic style of beauty, which generally softened the hearts of those who were most ill disposed towards her. And her husband was no more insensible to the charm of her loveliness than to the appeal made to his pity by her tears. At the same time he was inclined to say to himself that she was unjust when she accused him of risking nothing for her sake. He thought that he had risked a good deal. For the world called him a proud man ; and yet he had married his mother's waiting-maid, and then carefully concealed the marriage.

His dark handsome face, with its boldly-marked features, heavy moustache, and stern black brows, from beneath which a pair of fine dark eyes looked somewhat scornfully and stormily out upon the world, wore no well-pleased expression as Lucy poured forth her complaints. He said nothing at first, but moved the papers before him restlessly with his right hand as she proceeded.

"It will kill me, Gaston! This secrecy, these years of waiting! What do you hope to get by it? Why should we not let everybody know, and face the storm that would follow? Are you *afraid* of what your mother and your brother will say? Are you *afraid* of what the world will say? Oh! why did you marry me at all if you are so ashamed of me?" A fresh burst of tears completed her appeal.

Mr. Ravenscroft threw himself back in his chair with a movement of impatience, but his face expressed perplexity rather than displeasure.

"Be reasonable, Lucy," he said. "This arrangement will not last much longer; and you know that it was made with your own consent."

"Yes, years ago," said Lucy passionately; "years ago, when I was a mere child, and did not understand the view that all the world would take of my position. You took me abroad, and I heard nothing—saw nothing—but what you chose me to see and hear. It was only when baby came that I began to understand; and as soon as we set foot in England, I knew—I——"

"Shall I take you back to Italy?" said her husband in a low voice.

"No; why should I go to Italy? I want to have my own place at home; I want the people at Netherby to know that I am your wife. What must they all think of me now? My foster-mother, and poor Davy, who was like a brother to me—I must have broken their hearts long ago. Oh, Gaston, be good to me; show me that you love me!"

"It seems," said Gaston, with a flash of his eyes, "that you prefer the good opinion of Mrs. Rowe and her son, the fiddler, to your husband's welfare. Have I not told you a hundred times that I must wait until I am independent of my people at home before I can tell them about our marriage? You never troubled me concerning it until our return to England six months ago. I wish to heaven that we had stayed in Italy!"

"Ah, yes!" cried Lucy, with resentful indignation—"that you might not have to think about your wife's rights and your wife's position. *They* did not matter—in Italy; she never claimed them there."

"And who has been suggesting to you that you should claim them here?" asked Mr. Ravenscroft sternly. "You had not these notions before our return, as you confess. Who has been talking to you, Lucy?"

Her face crimsoned, but her eyes did not fall beneath the keen gaze with which he confronted her.

"Nobody has been talking to me," she said.

"I don't believe you," he answered with sharp directness. Then he tossed away his papers, rose, and approached her. "Come," he said, putting his hands on her shoulders and compelling her to turn towards him, "tell me who it is. Some meddling fool, no doubt; let me hear."

"No one has been talking to me," she repeated.

"Somebody has been writing to you then, eh? I am right this time, it seems, from the flame in your cheeks. What a wretched quibble!" he added, with a distinct note of anger in his voice, as he released her and walked to the fireplace, where he rested his elbow on the mantelpiece and looked down upon his boy. "Why must a woman always have a mystery, I wonder?"

"My mystery is nothing to the one you are making," she said defiantly. "I would not conceal the fact of my marriage for a day if I had my own way."

"No, you would prefer to ruin me."

She tried to look haughtily offended, but her lip quivered. Gaston however did not glance towards her. He held out his hand to the little boy who was now clinging to his knee, and babbling baby nonsense to him in an undertone. Lucy suddenly rose and pressed her hands to her ears.

" What a noise the child makes!" she said irritably. " If you are not going to listen to me any longer, Gaston——"

"Pardon me: I am not only going to listen to you, but to say something which will require your closest attention," said her husband in a tone of dry courtesy. " If you will kindly wait for one moment I will take Bertie to his nurse. He is rather too old now to listen to the wrangling of his parents."

He stooped down and took the child into his arms. The boy shouted with delight: his little hands were thrust into his father's short black locks, and his little feet drummed gaily on his father's broad chest as he was carried from the room. But his joy was changed to wailing when he found that he was consigned to his nurse's care after an unusually short ride. With both little arms he clung to his father's neck; it was with some difficulty, and after repeated and tender embraces, that Gaston disengaged himself. " I'll come back soon; be a man, Bertie; don't cry," he said. " I must go and talk to mamma."

His manner with the child was wonderfully soft and caressing: he had no imperious ways with Bertie, though he might be lavish of them in his intercourse with other people. Lucy Ravenscroft, sitting alone where he had left her, said to herself with a touch of added bitterness:

" There is no question about his love for the child. The only doubt is whether he has any love for me. If he had, he could bear to sacrifice a little money for my sake."

When Gaston Ravenscroft returned he saw from her face and attitude that she was in no compliant mood. His own brow grew dark as he took up a position on the hearthrug and addressed her.

" The sooner we come to an understanding the better, Lucy. We have been married some time, and I don't see why you should have so completely changed your tone during the last few months with respect to your position. For four years you have been my wife. If I have not chosen to write to my mother and my brother about you, or to take you to Netherby, I have acted only out of consideration for you. If I tell them, don't you know what will happen? My mother has unlimited control over her own fortune: I am entirely dependent upon her; and she would never give me another penny if she knew of our marriage. I am sorry if this sounds brutal; but it is the truth."

"In fact," said his wife, without looking at him, "we are living on an income obtained on false pretences. I should prefer honest poverty if I were you."

A red flush mounted to Gaston's forehead; he had some difficulty in answering calmly.

"I wish that I had told my mother from the beginning," he said. "But you know the circumstances as well as I do. I am taking from her hands only what my father left me by the will which he never signed. It would be mere cruel caprice if she deprived me of it—and yet she has the legal power to do so, and would doubtless use it if she had a fair excuse." He spoke very bitterly. "I think it is hard enough that I should have to accept it in this way without your upbraiding me for the concealment of our marriage, Lucy."

"If I were a man," said she with some sullenness, "I would have made a career for myself and dispensed with my mother's help by this time. I would have made myself free to tell the world that I had a son, even if I did not wish to acknowledge the boy's mother."

"And pray, what more could I do than I have done?" said Gaston, a dangerous gleam appearing in his eyes. "As long as I lived abroad I scarcely touched my mother's money; I spent my own, and hoped that I should get some appointment which would keep me. But now I have nothing to do, and I have spent my own paltry two thousand—how can we live without my mother's money? As soon as I can—that is, as soon as I get some work—I will make a clean breast of it and give up all the Netherby connection, Lucy; but till then, for your own sake, I mean to say nothing."

“Then I shall tell the truth.　I will not be a mark for slander and ignominy any longer.”

“If you were slandered I should be the first to protect you; but you are not slandered,” said Gaston coolly.　“Just look at the facts of the case.　My mother and I seldom corresponded when I was abroad : in that obscure little place where we lived we saw nobody who would think it worth while to inform her of your existence. And here—in an equally obscure place—our very name is unknown.　My letters are forwarded to me under cover from London.　How can slander be busy about you ?　The thing is impossible. Nobody knows that I am here : nobody guesses that you are here with me.　Just keep quiet, and when the proper time comes I will take care that you receive the treatment due to you as my wife.”

“You say that nobody knows that you are here,” said Lucy quickly.　“Do you call Captain Harcourt nobody ?”

“Is it Captain Harcourt that I have to thank for the change in your manner towards me ?” Gaston asked in the iciest of tones.

“No.”　　But Lucy blushed and hesitated.

"He seemed so surprised—when he came first," she added in a low voice. "I did not like it."

"He shall not come here again."

"Oh yes, he shall—he must. You cannot forbid him the house."

"I both can and will."

"You do everything you can to make me miserable!" said Mrs. Ravenscroft, suddenly burying her face in her hands and bursting into tears. "I wish that I was back in old Hester Rowe's cottage or at work on your mother's dresses: I was far happier then than I am now."

Gaston looked at her with a frown of despairing bewilderment. A woman would have seen at a glance that Lucy was far from strong, and that her present state of mind and body was one that required careful management. But Gaston Ravenscroft had no clue to the reason for her bursts of temper and hysterical passion: she was sensitively reticent on the subject of her bodily ailments, and left him to conclude that she was losing the gentleness and good humour which had always characterised her in earlier days. He even fancied that she was weeping over the banishment of Captain Harcourt—a friend of his own who had recently appeared in the neighbourhood and accidentally discovered Gaston's place of residence, and an angry frown disfigured his face at this supposition.

"What is it that you do want?" he said rather bitterly. "My mother's recognition? What good would it do you? It is no use crying, Lucy; I can't do anything at present. I should bring a crowd of duns down on my head if they knew that I had married, and all hope of help from Netherby would be gone. Wait till I get an appointment. I have one promised. It is only a question of weeks now."

"I have waited long enough. I will wait no longer."

"Indeed! And pray what will you do?"

"I will write to your mother myself. I will write to the Rowes."

"You will do nothing of the kind."

"I will." She raised her head and looked him defiantly in the face. "I will either have the marriage declared, or I will leave you altogether."

Gaston shrugged his shoulders. "I wish you

would not talk like a fool, Lucy," he said, in a tone which showed that this threat was not now made for the first time. "I'll do what I can; but you must have patience."

"No," she answered him; "I am tired of having patience. I sometimes think that you mean to keep me in the background all your life. Why do you treat me in this way? I have not made a mistake, have I? I *am* your wife, Gaston? Why can you not say so to the world?"

"Good heavens!" said Gaston, moving impatiently to the door; "am I continually to rehearse the reasons for my conduct, Lucy? You know them as well as I do. You seem to have exceedingly little trust in me when you speak in this way. Now understand, once and for all, that I will hear no more of this nonsense. Of course if you choose to ruin me for life you can do so; but in that case——"

"Well, in that case?" she said, rising as he laid his hand upon the door-handle, and advancing a step or two towards him with crimsoning cheeks and flashing eyes: "supposing that I do tell the truth and ruin you—as you call it—what then?"

He paused for a moment. She had roused his temper, never a very placable one, and there was a dangerous look upon his face—the look of a man whose impulses were uncontrolled, and whose will had seldom been resisted.

" In that case," he said sternly, " the less you ventured into my presence afterwards the better. I would never speak to you again."

Then he went out, shutting the door sharply behind him. He was hot, angry, excited : it took him full three-quarters of an hour's smoking and walking over the downs to bring him back to a gentler frame of mind. But at last he acknowledged to himself that, although Lucy had been provoking, she had had right upon her side, and he was sorry for his harsh words to her. If she disobeyed him a thousand times he knew that he should forgive her after all. His declaration that he would never speak to her again if she told her story was a mere expression of anger which she must take for what it was worth. She understood him and she loved him. He would go back to the house and make it up with her. But he could not risk the future for the sake of a woman's whim, he told himself.

He was sorry now that he had not made his marriage known from the beginning; he had never meant the concealment to last so long, but since the secret had been kept until now, he must not precipitate matters by divulging it too suddenly.

He knew afterwards that to have made a secret at all of his marriage had been a great—in some respects a fatal—error. Deceit had been very easy in the first instance, but it was not so easy to rid himself of its consequences. He paid dearly in after years for his mistake.

He had turned homewards, but was yet distant from his house, when a boy from the railway-station met him and delivered a telegram which had just arrived. He found that it was from an old college friend who besought him to come at once to London, as he had secured for him an interview with an official personage which might be of great service to him. The interview, however, was fixed for that afternoon, and he must start at once if he wished to avail himself of the opportunity.

Mr. Ravenscroft consulted a time-table card, and found that he had only a quarter of an hour

in which to catch the train. An explanation
with Lucy was impossible. He could but send
her a message and make the best of his way to
town. He wrote a few words on the blank leaf
of a note-book, and gave it to the boy with a
shilling, telling him to deliver that paper at once
to the lady at the cottage. The boy promised
to take the note; and Gaston set off for the
railway-station with an easy mind.

He caught the London train. But the boy
to whom his written message had been confided
happened to meet a friend, in whose company
the shilling was rapidly expended upon apples
and ginger-beer; and at the close of the repast
the folded scrap of paper was mysteriously
missing. Master Bob Stokes had managed to
lose it on the way; and Lucy Ravenscroft never
received her husband's letter.

CHAPTER II.

DESERTED.

WHEN Mr. Ravenscroft had left the house, his wife drew a letter from her pocket and began to pore over it with curious intentness. His guess had been in the main correct: somebody had been writing to her and putting into her mind suspicions that would never have entered it of their own accord. But she could not have told him the name of her correspondent, for she did not know it. The letter was an anonymous one, and it was one of a series which she had received at intervals since her return to England. They had always been delivered to her by hand when Gaston was out; and the messenger had generally been either a child or a labouring man, who professed to know nothing of the person from whom the letters came.

The circumstances of Gaston's marriage may here be briefly told. He was the second son of a large landholder in Lincolnshire, who died when his two boys were mere children. Their mother had speedily married again,—this time a certain Baron Waldstein, with whom she lived for many years at Vienna,—and the boys were left at school, spending their holidays with a cousin of their mother, a Mr. Hervey, whose residence was close to their own. In course of time Philip Ravenscroft, the elder of the brothers, grew up, took the management of affairs into his own hands, and married. Gaston, who had been left with next to no fortune more from accident than design, lived a somewhat idle life in London when his school-days were over, in the hope of a vaguely-promised appointment which never came, and seldom visited Ravenscroft Hall, his brother's house at Netherby. His mother, however, being again widowed and partially disabled by a slight paralytic seizure, returned to her old home in Lincolnshire, and Gaston felt it his duty to present himself sometimes to her notice. He never got on well with her; she seemed to reserve all her affection for her elder son, Philip:

but he tried hard to be patient and respectful, even when she tried his temper, as she often did, by contemptuous gibes at his awkwardness, his roughness, his want of *savoir faire.* In return she made him an allowance, without which he would have found it singularly hard to meet his expenses. For Gaston Ravenscroft was a man who contrived to get through a great deal of money without much to show for it at the end.

During one of his visits to Netherby he formed a slight acquaintance with a very pretty village girl named Lucy Moore. She had been brought up by a woman of half-gipsy origin, named Hester Rowe; but her parents—simple, honest people — had lived and died as small tradesfolk in Netherby. Gaston had known Hester Rowe and her lame son Davy, who played the violin and mended shoes, and pretty Lucy Moore herself for years; but he was specially attracted to the girl in her bloom of seventeen, and was half vexed, half pleased, when he found that she had accepted the situation of lady's maid to his mother. He saw her daily : he fell in love with her and she with him; and in the end she went away with him, and they were married at an obscure little church in London when she was barely eighteen and he was twenty-one.

It was essential to Gaston's plans that nobody should know of his marriage. Everybody believed that Lucy had been led by him to leave her home, and for a time there was a buzz of excitement and suspicion in the village; but Gaston stayed away until the rumours subsided, and refused to answer any questions respecting Lucy's fate. When his relations questioned him on the subject he even gave them clearly to understand that his business was not theirs, and that he would tell them nothing either about Lucy or about himself.

His mother was not difficult to silence. He knew that he could not blind her; her shrewd and cynical eyes saw through all his evasions; but she did not pester him with questions. As he had reason to think in later years, what the Baroness Waldstein wished to know she would learn for herself by fair means or by foul, with his permission or without it. It was possible that she knew the whole story from beginning to end, even when Gaston flattered himself that he was most sedulously hiding it from her. But if she knew it, she knew also how to hold her peace.

He took his wife away with him to Italy soon after the marriage. He never meant to keep it a secret for very long; he believed himself sure of an appointment which should lift him above the necessity of consulting the wishes of his family: but months and years went on, and the opportunity of declaring his marriage never came. In Italy he almost forgot that such a declaration was a duty; but as soon as they returned to England Lucy began, for the first time, to manifest an eager desire to assume her position in public as his wife, and to see her boy acknowledged as Gaston Ravenscroft's lawful son. And this desire had been first created and then stimulated by the succession of anonymous letters which had come into her hands; letters which suggested horrible suspicions of Gaston's good faith, and caused her to display towards him at times an amount of bitterness and jealous feeling of which she herself was afterwards ashamed.

She longed above all things to let it be known at Netherby that she was Gaston's wife. There were her own people, as she still fondly called them, Hester Rowe and Davy the cripple, for whom she entertained a warm and yearning affection. She had been allowed to enter into no correspondence with them since the day of her departure from the village, and she longed to set their minds at rest concerning her fate. There were the Baroness whom she had served, and Philip Ravenscroft her son; both of these had treated her with a cold distrust and haughtiness of manner, which it still made her cheeks burn to remember. Philip Ravenscroft's wife, Felicia, had been gentle and kind enough; but of her Lucy was perhaps more afraid than of the Baroness. She felt also that she should like to justify herself and Gaston in Mr. Hervey's eyes. He was a man of cold smooth ways and tones, a man whom Gaston deeply disliked; and yet Lucy knew, by instinct, that her husband felt lowered in his own eyes by his inability to explain away the suspicions which Richard Hervey —his cousin and former guardian—had conceived of him.

But it was only since her arrival in England that Lucy had had such thoughts as these. In

Italy she had been as happy and contented as a child. But those peaceful days of her early married life were past; she had changed from a trustful girl into an exacting and imperious woman. It was her love for her boy rather than mere womanly pride that worked this change; but the change was a great one and was destined to lead to sad results.

As she sat alone after Gaston's departure, she drew forth once more the last letter that she had received from her unknown correspondent, and pondered over it with aching heart and burning eyes.

" You have not then prevailed ?"—so ran the words. " You have not persuaded Gaston Ravenscroft to acknowledge you as his wife ? No, and you never will. He keeps you in the background, because he is ashamed of your birth and your want of education; and if you do not stand up for your own rights nobody else will. If he were to die, what proofs have you to show his family that he ever made you his wife at all ?"

Lucy meditated much over these last words. She scarcely realised the value of a marriage

certificate or of the register kept in the parish
where her marriage had taken place ; but she
had a vague notion that her "lines," as she
called them, were in Gaston's possession,—not in
her own,—and that if she could find them, they
would give her greater confidence in her position.
She rose tremblingly from her seat and began to
wonder whether Gaston carried them upon his
person or whether they were in his desk, of
which the keys had been that morning carelessly
flung upon the dressing-table. She resolved to
ascertain this fact for herself.

Her suspicions of Gaston were entirely un-
founded. He had acted with utter recklessness
in the first instance, as he always did when he
set his heart upon any object ; and his first reck-
less act had, in his opinion, needed concealment.
It was this concealment that troubled and perplexed him now as much as it fretted Lucy, but
in a different way. He knew that there would
never be any difficulty in proving the legality of
the marriage whether he were alive or dead : he
had made every provision for the establishment
of his wife's position when she or he should find
it necessary to put forward her claim ; but he

never thought of saying so to her. He could not have believed that Lucy would suspect him of a dishonourable motive for his silence. He thought that she had perfect trust in him—and he was mistaken.

The papers that Lucy sought were easily found. They were placed in a secret drawer, which he himself had shown her how to open. She took them out—precious papers they were to her—the certificate of her marriage, of the boy's birth and baptism, and with them a lock of Bertie's hair when he was yet a baby, and a withered rose which she herself had given to her husband years ago. These relics failed to soften her as they ought to have done. She put back the rose and the lock of hair with hurried, trembling fingers, but she kept the papers in her own possession. Then she went downstairs again, feeling less anxious than before, but more than ever resolved to insist upon her rights.

She waited indoors for Gaston. She expected him to come to her subdued and penitent and wretched, as was his wont after a quarrel. But time passed on, and Gaston did not return. At noon she began to feel uneasy. When the luncheon hour arrived and he was still absent, she felt not only uneasy but afraid. She had never known him to be so angry before as to stay away from her for three hours at a time.

Gaston, as we know, was already well on his way to London. The telegraph boy, having finished his game and spent his shilling, was bethinking himself of the paper which he had been charged to deliver at the little house in the hollow, and was becoming somewhat alarmed at the discovery that the paper was altogether missing. And Mrs. Ravenscroft was working herself up into a tempest of rage and grief and suspicion, which would neither let her eat nor sit still nor behave like any rational creature at all.

In the course of the afternoon she departed from her usual custom so far as to walk to Elmstone, a distance of two miles, in order to see for herself whether he might not be strolling about the streets or sitting in the public reading-room. But he was, of course, nowhere to be seen. Then, as the afternoon drew to a close, she wended her weary way to the railway-station and made cautious inquiries of the clerk and porters. Had they that day seen the gentleman who lived at the Laurels? What was he like? Oh, a very tall gentleman, with a black moustache; very good-looking. His name? Mr. Croft. Yes, they had seen Mr. Croft (for this was the name under which Gaston was known in the neighbourhood); he had taken the up train to town at 11.15. He would be at Victoria station by one o'clock.

Lucy's limbs almost gave way beneath her as she heard these words. She was obliged to go into the waiting-room and drink some water before she could turn her face homewards. Gaston's sudden departure was entirely inexplicable to her, save on the ground of deep displeasure with her proceedings. If she had had his note she would easily have understood the whole matter; but, as neither note nor message reached her, she had no clue to any reason for his disappearance. She cried bitterly as she made her way across the wind-swept downs; and when she arrived at the house she was so much exhausted, so wan and worn by fatigue and tears and hunger (for she had tasted nothing since the morning, and had walked for some hours), that she was already the mere ghost of her ordinary self.

About eight o'clock in the evening a ring at the front door made her start up nervously. It could not be Gaston; he would never ring to announce his coming; but it might be a letter or a message that would explain everything. She dared not rush to the door; she stood erect in the middle of the room, her hands clasped, her face white, her eyes strained and gleaming—a sad yet lovely picture of expectation and distress at which the entering visitor stood amazed,—for it was nobody at all but Captain Harcourt, the young man who had claimed Gaston Ravenscroft's acquaintance, and had been to some extent taken into his confidence.

As he paused near the door, Lucy made a sudden movement which brought her close to the sofa, on which little Bertie was reposing in the serene soft sleep of childhood. The mother had felt that she could not bear to be alone; she had brought her boy downstairs from his crib and tucked him up warmly and safely in a corner of the old-fashioned broad flat couch. She stood with her hand upon the cushions that formed his pillow and looked—not at Harcourt, but beyond him, as though she expected to see him followed by another. But Captain Harcourt was alone.

"Why—why have you come?" were the words that rose to Lucy's lips. "You have bad news, bad news of Gaston?"

The young man's face expressed genuine astonishment and dismay.

"Bad news!" he stammered. "Bad news, Mrs. Ravenscroft! I have no news at all."

"Not of Gaston? Have you not seen him? Have you heard nothing of him at all?"

"Yes," said Harcourt with an embarrassed laugh; "I have certainly seen something of him, but he seemed well enough as far as I could judge. He——"

"Where did you see him?" she interposed, with an eager light in her eyes.

"Well, I have just come up from Queensborough myself," said the young fellow, speaking confusedly, for he had a vague sense that everything was going wrong in the Ravenscroft household, and began to feel very sorry that he had ventured to call on pretty Mrs. Ravenscroft that evening. "Just come from Queensborough, and knowing that you would be alone, I——"

"And how did you know that I should be alone?" said Lucy, growing whiter than she had even been before.

"Knew! Oh, why, Mrs. Ravenscroft, I did not think that your husband could fly back from the Continent on the wings of the wind! I saw him on board, you know," said the young man, wagging his honest foolish head at the anxious wife, with a smile that looked to her like one of mockery, though it was in reality only one of sheer awkwardness and confusion, "on board the Flushing boat——"

"The Flushing boat!" It seemed to Lucy that the room was growing dark, that Captain Harcourt's voice was strangely distant, and that the floor was shaking beneath her feet; but she only looked towards the bearer of ill tidings with a ghastly sort of smile, and vaguely repeated his last words. "The Flushing boat?" she said. "Yes — the Flushing boat!"

"He said you knew that he would be away— that you were not expecting him to return,"

Captain Harcourt proceeded uncertainly. "He said you knew all about it——"

"Oh yes," said Lucy from between her gasping lips. "Of course I knew—I——"

She did not finish the sentence. She gave a little cry and fell down upon the floor beside Bertie's couch, and lay there, a tumbled heap of white clothes, and a face as white as they. For the moment Captain Harcourt thought that she was dead.

An unexpected thing had happened to Gaston Ravenscroft. His interview with the great official personage had terminated very satisfactorily, and when he came away from Downing Street he began to please himself with the reflection that he should soon be completely independent of help from his relations, and that he could therefore make known his marriage with Lucy. He turned into his club in order to see whether any letters were waiting for him, and there he found not only letters but a telegram. He tore it open, and read the message with surprise, succeeded by alarm and sorrow. It was from his sister-in-law, Felicia Ravenscroft. She telegraphed from Wiesbaden, whither she with her husband had gone for a few weeks' holiday. Philip Ravenscroft had been thrown from his horse and injured so seriously that his life could hardly be prolonged over the morrow. Gaston was entreated to come at once to Wiesbaden if he wished to see Philip again alive.

There was just time, he found, to make hasty preparations for a journey, and to catch the train to Queensborough, whence a boat left for Flushing that afternoon. He did not telegraph to Lucy, thinking that she knew already of his visit to London, and that she would not expect him for a couple of days. There was no need to startle her by a telegram. He would write a note to her whilst on board, and post it as soon as he reached Flushing. He did not know what other agencies were at work, nor how his absence would be interpreted by the foolish, jealous little heart of the woman whom he had left behind. As it happened, he did not post his letter until he reached Wiesbaden ; but this additional delay mattered very little. The mischief was done.

Philip Ravenscroft and his brother had never been on intimate terms. Their natures were too dissimilar to amalgamate. Philip was a man of cold and cautious temperament—a dabbler in art, a profound believer in the conventional canons of society. He looked upon Gaston's fiery and emotional nature with a feeling akin to contempt, certainly with grave disapproval. Nevertheless, Gaston, who had far more affection for Philip than Philip had for him, was sincerely distressed, and even overwhelmed by grief at his elder brother's death, and at the desolation brought upon the poor young widow with her one little daughter. The bitterness of the bereavement was not in the slightest degree alleviated to him by the fact that, as Philip left no son, he was now the head of the house, and master of the greater portion of the Ravenscroft property. But for his wife and child he could heartily have wished himself no gainer by his brother's death; but for them he would almost have offered to hand over the estate to Mrs. Philip Ravenscroft and little Olivia. It did give him a thrill of relief (for which he angrily blamed himself) to know that he need no longer keep secret the history of his marriage. The secrecy and deceit which had embittered his life for the last four years might now come to an end.

He wrote two or three lines to Lucy, and was surprised to receive no answer from her; but he was too much absorbed by the care of his sister-in-law and the arrangements for Philip's funeral to think very much about his wife's silence. She was no great letter-writer at the best of times : he would explain everything to her when he returned to Elmstone.

Some days elapsed before that return took place. Felicia could not be left alone : she was already ill with grief and fatigue. Gaston travelled with her to Netherby, and saw his mother for a few minutes only before he went back to London and thence to Elmstone.

He reached Elmstone at dusk. As he approached his own house he noticed that it presented a curiously desolate appearance; the rooms were unlighted, and the gate was locked. The solitary maid-servant came out to admit him, and looked inquisitively into his face.

" Your mistress is in ?" Gaston said quickly.

" Oh no, sir. She has not got back yet, sir, you know."

"Not got back? What do you mean?" said Gaston, with a sudden thrill of dismay. "Where has she gone?"

"I don't know, sir. She has not been here for a fortnight."

"A fortnight!"

"She left here with Master Bertie, sir, on the day after you went away. I don't know where she has gone. I thought that she went to you."

Gaston stood amazed. "Did she leave no letter or message?" he asked, after a moment's pause.

"No, sir," said the maid, demurely observant of his agitation. "She left no letter or message for any one. She went to the railway-station without any luggage except a little bag,—and Captain Harcourt went with her."

Gaston went to seek Captain Harcourt. But he had vanished from the town, and left not a trace behind.

CHAPTER III.

THE WIFE.

In Gaston's first frenzy of anger and astonishment a terrible suspicion presented itself to his mind. He thought that Lucy had run away from him in company with a lover, and that this lover was Edmund Harcourt. It need hardly be said that this conjecture was founded upon nothing in Lucy's previous conduct or character. And Lucy's love for her husband had never been greater than it was upon the day when she left her home at Elmstone.

Captain Harcourt's information that Gaston had left England, together with the absence of any message or letter to that effect, made poor Lucy believe one of two things: either that Gaston was so much displeased with her that he had resolved to punish her by going abroad for a holiday without informing her of his intention —an explanation much too simple to be readily accepted by Lucy's fevered mind; or (and for this idea the anonymous letters were to blame) that he had grown tired of her and meant never to return. On recovering from the swoon into which she had fallen upon hearing Captain Harcourt's words, she awoke to a sense of maddening uncertainty. And, to make matters worse, on the morning after Gaston's departure there came for her, no letter from Gaston, but another of those stinging unsigned communications which, if she had been a sensible woman, she would have thrown into the fire unread. But she was not a sensible woman; and she read the letter with a feeling of pain and humiliation that seemed to scorch her.

"Did you ever ask whether you had been married properly at all? This letter is from one who wishes you well and is sorry to see you so deceived. When Gaston Ravenscroft is away from you he boasts of the trick he played you in London. Mark my words; you are not his wife, and that is why he hides you from the world. If he had really married you he would not be so slow to acknowledge the fact. And, unless you yourself do not feel sure about the legality of the marriage, why do *you* not make it known? If you have any rights, claim them at once."

"I *will* claim them," said Lucy, turning very white as she read the words. "I have been foolish and weak. If those papers mean anything, I am Gaston's wife; and I will say so— to his mother—to the Rowes—to every one. We will have no more secrecy—for Bertie's sake!"

Forthwith she made her preparations. She would go to Netherby, and she would see the Baroness herself. She would tell her, and she would tell her kind old friends the Rowes, and Mr. Hervey at the Manor, and everybody else whom it might concern, that she was Gaston's wife. Thus, if it were not true, she would force the truth from Gaston's lips. Thus she would take her revenge upon him for his cruel conduct in going away and leaving her without a word.

Captain Harcourt called to inquire after her health when she was on the point of leaving the house. He walked to the station with her, good-humouredly carrying Bertie, and taking the railway ticket for her to London. It was then only, seeing how ill and worn she looked, that he invented an excuse for going up to London by the same train, simply that he might be at hand to assist his friend's wife if she should want him. He did not travel in the same carriage with her; and Lucy was hardly conscious of his intention until the train had started. At the terminus he reappeared, ready to secure a cab for her or do anything that she might need doing. She was only eager for his departure; she did not want anybody " to spy upon her," as she expressed it to herself; and she was relieved when she found herself and her boy in the cab, with Captain Harcourt's honest, puzzled face turned mutely towards her from the pavement, as she drove away to King's Cross Station.

When she reached the station and put her hand into her pocket for her purse, she made the startling discovery that she had lost it—probably left it behind in the railway carriage. She had, however, sufficient loose silver with her to pay the cabman; then she betook herself to the ladies' waiting-room and counted the coins that remained. She found that she had enough money to pay for a third-class ticket to a station some five miles distant from Netherby. She knew the station well; she had often walked from it to her own home in the days of her girlhood. She could walk that distance easily, she considered, forgetting that what had seemed easy in those days might be more difficult to her now that she was a woman in delicate health, with a child of three years old clinging to her hand. Should she go forward, or should she go back to Elmstone and await Gaston's return? Ah, perhaps Gaston never would return! She would go on, at any cost, to Netherby.

But before she was far upon her way she regretted her decision. She had not been well for some weeks; fatigue, anxiety, and exhaustion now began to make themselves felt. From time to time she grew sick and faint; she began to wonder how she should reach the end of the journey, how she should walk those five long miles that lay between the station and the village of Netherby. In Netherby itself she did not think that she should want for friends or for assistance.

She was deadly pale when she left the carriage at the station to which she had taken her ticket; her limbs trembled and her eyes were dim. Bertie was crying wearily; she spent her last coin in some biscuits and a glass of milk for him, drank some water herself and set out upon her way.

For a time she felt stronger, and walked rapidly. She left the high road for the grassy lanes and meadows which formed a " short cut " to Netherby; she had ascertained at the station that the way was unaltered still, and she knew that she remembered every step of it. She hastened therefore, for the afternoon was growing late and the clouds were gathering overhead. She began to wish that she had left Bertie behind. A storm would not hurt her : it might frighten him and make him ill. The first few drops of rain that fell aroused in her a sensation of defeat and dismay which proved how greatly she had lost heart since she set out that morning.

She tried to hasten her footsteps. But she was growing sadly exhausted: the feverish strength which had at first animated her had given way, and she was conscious of bodily pain and weakness. She sat down under a tree for a little time, but soon rose and stumbled on for a few paces, then seated herself again on the wet grass, regardless of the pouring rain and of Bertie's wailing cries. She began to understand how much she had risked in this wild endeavour to vindicate her rights. But now it was too late to retrace her steps ; she must go on with the work that she had begun—on to the very end.

Her progress was necessarily slow. She walked a few steps only at a time and at long intervals. It was wonderful that she did not miss her way altogether or lie down by the way-side and lapse into insensibility. There were no buildings upon the road which she had chosen; and if there had been, it is doubtful whether she would have found sufficient energy to ask for help. How she managed to stagger on for nearly five weary miles amidst the gathering darkness, with a child crying at her side and the rain beating in her face, could never be told. Cer-tainly she achieved the greater part of her peril-ous journey, for at ten o'clock that night she was found lying in a lane near Netherby Church, not far from Mrs. Rowe's cottage, with Bertie at her side. She had left the railway-station at five o'clock in the afternoon.

The person who found her was a broad-shouldered, undersized man, with a limp in his walk. He was making his way along the lane to Mrs. Rowe's lonely cottage, with a violin-case slung upon his back and a thick stick in his hand. He had a rough, ugly, thick-featured face, a shock of dark hair, and a pair of dark deep-set eyes, through which looked out into the world as true and loving and generous a soul as ever God had made. This man had cherished a silent love for Lucy from the days of her childhood; and she had tricked and abandoned him as soon as Gaston Ravenscroft had become her lover. It was the fiddler of whom Gaston had spoken contemptu-ously to his wife—David Rowe, whose mother had given her a home when she was left an orphan.

This man bent over her, thinking at first that she was some beggar woman who had fallen in the lane. Her clothes were so drenched with rain and stained with mud that, indeed, she looked no better than a tramp from the nearest workhouse. Bertie roused himself from a semi-slumber, and began his despairing wail once more. And then David Rowe saw the supposed beggar woman's face and knew that it was the face of the woman whom he had loved.

He uttered a wild, inarticulate cry, knelt down beside her and began to chafe her cold fingers and call her by her name. She moved a little and moaned feebly, but did not open her eyes. It was evident that she was quite unconscious.

David Rowe stopped rubbing her hands at last, and looked into her white drawn face. The rain-drops fell upon it as he looked ; the wind whistled in the branches of the elm-trees overhead. The child, standing beside him, and clutching the fiddler's arm as if in fear lest he should leave him alone with his mother in the darkness and the cold, burst forth once more into piteous sobs and tears.

The man rose, shaking off the child's hand as if he could not bear that touch. Then he managed—not without difficulty, although he was of great muscular strength—to lift the insensible woman from the ground and carry her in his arms for the few yards that intervened between her resting-place and Hester Rowe's cottage. The little boy ran sobbing at his heels; David Rowe took no notice of him as he strode along the muddy lane, with the frail and precious burden in his arms.

He struck a blow with his foot against the cottage door. It was opened immediately by a gray-haired woman, with a stern, handsome, old face, singularly unlike his own. She held a candle in her hand, and raised it so as to throw its light full upon his face as she spoke to him.

"You!" she said. "I had given you up for to-night. You are late. What have you got there?"

"Lucy," he answered briefly. "Let us in."

The candle flickered. The woman's hand trembled, but she resolutely barred the way.

"Take her back to the place where you found her, and let her lie," she said, in harsh and bitter tones. "I gave her up years ago—when she gave us up; there is no home for her here."

"Wherever my home is, hers shall be," said her son sternly. "Turn her away and you turn me away too."

"Is that her child?" said Mrs. Rowe, catching sight of the little boy. "I expected as much. Let them go to the workhouse, both of them."

"Do you wish to see her die in my arms?" said David Rowe. "She's ill, she's poor, she's in trouble; let her in, or her blood will lie on your head. Mother, you used not to be so hard on those that had seen trouble. Let me bring her in, or, by the Lord, you shall never see my face again!"

His voice rose as he spoke, and Lucy writhed and moaned in his arms as though she understood. The old woman was silent for a moment, then drew back from the door.

"You must have your way," she said, with a kind of cold dignity. "Lucy Moore broke your heart and ruined your life, as well as her own, perhaps; but now that she is homeless and friendless, as it seems, you must needs shelter her under your roof, and share your last bit and sup with her. Do as you please; I will not say you nay."

Davy entered, and laid his burden gently upon a bed that stood at one side of the dimly-lighted room. The child followed him. Mrs. Rowe shut the cottage door, and stirred up the embers of the fire. And thus did Lucy return to the home that had been hers in days of yore.

Mrs. Rowe did not long hesitate to help David in his efforts for Lucy's restoration. She tried to warm her hands and bring her back to consciousness; she warmed milk and food for the little boy, and put him to bed; but she did everything with a grimness and a severity of aspect which said little for any kindliness of feeling towards the wanderers. When all her remedies had failed, she said to her son, with the same dryness of manner—

"You must go for the doctor. I can't do anything more for her. She is very ill."

Davy started up and went out of the house without a word of reply.

He returned after a time with the doctor. By this time the unconscious woman had been carried into an inner room. Davy remained alone in bitter anxiety and fear, which was by no means dissipated when he heard the doctor's report. Lucy was certainly very ill—dangerously ill, in fact; it was doubtful whether she could ever recover the strain that she had put upon herself during the last few hours.   There was little hope.

For three days Hester Rowe watched by Lucy's bedside.   She kept David out of the room for the most part, much against his will; but at times he stole in for a few minutes and listened with feelings of mingled rage and grief to the incoherent words in which Lucy betrayed the desolation of her own soul.   Poor Lucy! her words were gathered up and commented upon in silence by two listeners who gave to them the darkest interpretation that they could bear. When she cried upon Gaston and besought him not to leave her, not to be angry with her, not to hide her from her friends, what could they do but believe the worst of Gaston and the worst of her?   She spoke of the letters that had told her of " Gaston's falseness;" she talked vaguely of his leaving her " for ever;" in short, she conveyed to their minds the impression that she had been abandoned and betrayed, and that she had wandered back to Netherby in despair to take refuge with her adopted mother and brother in the little cottage by the churchyard gate.

" It will be better for her to die than to live,"

Hester said once to her son in reply to his inquiries, and Davy assented with a groan.

Several times in her delirium it was noticed that Lucy spoke of certain papers which she wished to show; and she would not be satisfied until a little packet of paper, which the doctor folded so as to satisfy her, was placed in her hands. With this packet she seemed content. Her own papers—the papers which she had taken from Gaston's desk—meanwhile lay in the long grass beneath the trees, in the place where she had been found, undiscovered and undisturbed. They had been placed in a leathern case, and were therefore to some degree protected from the effects of exposure to the weather; but unless they were speedily reclaimed there was every chance of their complete destruction.

The doctor's opinion was correct. On the third day after her arrival at Netherby, Lucy Ravenscroft lay cold and white and still upon the truckle-bed to which she had been carried; and beside her, cold and white and still as she, lay the infant who had breathed but for a few minutes before it closed its eyes in the sleep of death, into which its mother also fell. Lucy was dead. Gaston Ravenscroft, unconscious of his bereavement, was far away in a foreign land; little Bertram, stunned and frightened into silence by strange and hard surroundings, was left alone with two persons who had, perhaps not unreasonably under the circumstances, a positive aversion to his presence, and a desire to rid themselves of him as soon as possible.

David Rowe, a man of gentle and kindly nature, tried hard to be tender in thought and speech to the little lad; but, in spite of himself, he could hardly bear the sight of Lucy's child. He had loved her for many years, and the thought of her disgrace filled him with a greater woe than the knowledge of her death. But Hester Rowe was made of sterner stuff. She had loved Lucy too, in a cold self-contained way, although Lucy had been none of her own kith and kin, and she was indignant in her heart because Lucy had scorned her son David and brought herself to shame which the old woman could not pardon. Hester herself was of gipsy origin; but she had married a Scotchman of strict views, and although she never adopted his religious principles, they had had an effect upon her. She was a rigid believer in purity of life, and she had no sympathy with Lucy in her apparent fall. The child was an outcast, a disgrace; and Hester Rowe was by no means inclined to cherish it for Lucy's sake, as a woman of a softer nature might have been. Still less was she disposed to call upon Gaston Ravenscroft to maintain his son. " The less the child has to do with that bad man the better," she said, grimly eying the sleeping boy one evening, and speaking to David in cold dry tones. " I will let him know that Lucy is dead. If he wishes to make inquiry about the boy, he can do so."

" Do you mean to keep the child here ?" said David, looking up.

" I'll think about that after the funeral."

" I must go back to Stanger's to-morrow evening," said the fiddler, with a depressed air. Stanger was the name of a travelling theatrical manager in whose troupe David was enrolled. " I can't stay any longer; but if you want money for the child, let me know from time to time, and I'll send it you. Netherby won't see me again for many a long day."

"I shall not want any money," said Mrs. Rowe.

There was a look of dark purpose upon her face, which made her son restless and uneasy; but he did not ask what his mother meant to do with the little waif and stray.

CHAPTER IV.

THE CHILD.

Lucy Ravenscroft and her baby were buried in Netherby churchyard a week after her flight from Elmstone. David Rowe went back to his duties on the evening after the funeral. Little Bertram was left upon Hester's hands, and she found him a heavy burden. But she speedily took means to rid herself of it.

She heard of the bereavement that had fallen upon the Ravenscrofts. She heard that Gaston Ravenscroft would now become the head of the house: she knew that he would be rich and powerful; and she deliberated with herself for a time as to whether she would not appeal to him to take the child into his care. But Lucy's words on her dying bed seemed to show that Gaston had cast off both her and her child, and

Mrs. Rowe thought it unlikely in that case that he would acknowledge his paternity. She was not eager to do anything either for the child's good or for Gaston Ravenscroft's satisfaction; but she resolved that he should know at least what Lucy's fate had been. With this intent, she wrote a short letter to him, which ran as follows :—

"SIR—Lucy Moore and her infant died at my house on the 20th of May, and were buried in Netherby churchyard. The little boy remains with me; but if he is not soon claimed by his friends, I shall send him to Mickleham Workhouse. I have no desire to bring up another child, as I brought up Lucy Moore, to repay kindness with ingratitude.—HESTER ROWE."

She sent this epistle up to Ravenscroft Hall, and waited for a reply. A week passed before any notice was taken of it. As a matter of fact she did not expect it to be answered until Mr. Ravenscroft returned to Netherby; and it was a full fortnight before he brought Mrs. Philip Ravenscroft back to her home. Then, as we know, he stayed for a few hours only and set off once more for Elmstone, where he hoped to find his wife and receive an explanation of her long silence. It was, however, before the day of his flying visit to Netherby that Hester Rowe received an answer to her letter. But that answer did not come from Gaston Ravenscroft.

She was sitting, stonily quiet, as was her wont, before the fire in her cottage, about four o'clock in the afternoon, when the sound of wheels broke upon her meditations. A dog-cart had been driven down the lane, and was standing before her door. Mrs. Rowe cast a quick glance at little Bertie, who was amusing himself somewhat dismally in a corner with a broken toy, and rose to greet her visitor. She expected to see Mr. Ravenscroft: she was somewhat disappointed to find herself confronted only by Mr. Hervey of Netherby Manor.

But she remembered that Mr. Hervey was a cousin of the Ravenscroft family, and an intimate friend of the old lady at the Hall. Probably he had brought her a message from Mr. Ravenscroft. He was a magistrate, a poor-law guardian, a man of importance in the place: no doubt he had come to see whether matters could not be quietly and satisfactorily arranged.

He was a man of sixty years of age, white-haired, bland, gentle and courteous of tongue, yet with a certain coldness of expression which made him feared even by those whom he wished to conciliate. Many stories of his harshness towards his tenants and dependants were rife in the neighbourhood. Chief among them was an account of his behaviour to his only daughter, who had married against his will. She had run away from home with a German music-master, and Mr. Hervey had refused to see her or to speak to her again. Rumour said that the German music-master was dead, that she had fallen into poverty, that she and her child were starving; finally, that she had died of sorrow, and that the child had been adopted by its father's relations; but no one knew how much there was of truth in any of these assertions. Poor Mabel Hervey had never been seen in Netherby since the day when she and her husband tremblingly presented themselves before the master of Netherby Manor, in order to ask his forgiveness for their stolen marriage, and had been coldly but politely requested to leave the house. Mr. Hervey now lived alone, and de-

voted himself in a dilettante sort of way to litera-
ture and art; but neither man nor woman could
say that he had ever shown one trace of regret
for the conduct of his daughter, nor one sign of
sorrow for the loneliness of his home.

He entered the cottage abruptly, shot a keen
glance at the boy, as Mrs. Rowe herself had done,
and accosted the old woman with an ironical and
decidedly unpleasant smile.

"I suppose you thought that you were not
going to receive any answer to your letter," he
began. "It is better that it should be answered
by word of mouth than in writing, however. I
have come in Mr. Ravenscroft's place, to answer it."

"Mr. Ravenscroft showed you my letter?"
said Hester, in her usual indifferent manner.

"I saw it—yes, I saw your letter," Mr. Hervey
answered, seating himself and looking round the
cottage with carelessness equal to her own. "That
is the boy, I suppose? Handsome little fellow,
Mrs. Rowe. I wonder that you do not wish to
keep him and bring him up. A grandson like
that child would do you credit."

"You forget, sir, that Lucy Moore was not my
daughter."

"Ah yes, one does forget that, Mrs. Rowe. Naturally you have not much interest in a child whose very existence might be considered a disgrace."

"There are others who have got to consider that," said Mrs. Rowe coldly. "He has plenty of relations in the village—on his father's side—if they choose to acknowledge him."

"You seem very sure of that," said Mr. Hervey. "And pray, who told you the name of this boy's father or of his relations?"

He looked at her very keenly as he spoke, and Hester Rowe seemed troubled.

"It was pretty plain," she said after a moment's pause, "to any one who listened to Lucy on her deathbed."

"Ah! And what did Lucy say to you?"

"She did not say anything to me exactly. She was light-headed from the moment she spoke first within my doors to the moment of her death. But folks tell the truth when they are light-headed more readily sometimes than when they've got their senses."

"Very likely," said Mr. Hervey in a peculiarly suave manner. "But they also confound fact and fiction sometimes in a very singular way. She never recovered consciousness, did she? And she left no writing behind her—no papers?"

" No."

" Then I should like to know upon what grounds you think that this child has any claim upon Mr. Ravenscroft!" said the magistrate with some severity. " If the ravings of an abandoned girl in her last delirium are all your proof, I think that you had much better hold your tongue, Mrs. Rowe, or you will find yourself in trouble."

" I've no wish to meddle or make in the matter," returned Hester monotonously. " I only go by what Lucy Moore said on her dying bed. She talked of nothing but ' Gaston,' ' Gaston ' all the time; and how he had left her and broken her heart and all the rest of it. It's natural enough that I should think that he was the man as ought to provide for the child."

" He won't do that."

" Is that what you've come to say, sir?"

" Yes, my good woman, it's that."

" Then the child must go to the workhouse," said Hester Rowe.

"Yes," rejoined Mr. Hervey dryly, "he must go to the workhouse, certainly."

There was a little silence. Mr. Hervey turned towards the boy, who, unconscious that his whole future life was shaped for him in that moment, had dragged his toy-cart into the centre of the floor and sat triumphant in a patch of sunlight which turned the brown of his curls to gold. He caught Mr. Hervey's eye, and laughed with babyish glee as the old man beckoned to him with his long-fingered finely-shaped white hand.

"Come to me," Mr. Hervey said. "Will you come?"

The boy rose and trotted fearlessly towards him.

"What is your name, little man?"

"Bertie."

"And your other name? What else beside Bertie?"

The child shook his head. "Mammy knows," he said regretfully, "but she wouldn't tell me. And now she's gone away."

"Will you come with me?"

"No," said Bertie stoutly.

" Why not ? "

" Me wait here till mammy come back again."

" But if I take you to see her ?——"

Mr. Hervey paused, half regretting the untruth ; for the child dropped the cart, which hitherto he had been holding tightly in his hand, and placed his fingers on Mr. Hervey's knee. " Yes," he said decidedly. " Me go with you to find mammy—now. And papa—and Rover— and everybody."

Mr. Hervey's hand closed, as it were involuntarily, over the soft little fingers on his knee. He looked at Mrs. Rowe with an odd smile.

" If you will not keep him, Mrs. Rowe," he said, " he might as well come away with me at once. I am going to Mickleham. I can see him to the workhouse on my way. I assure you that Mr. Ravenscroft will do nothing for him, and as you refuse to burden yourself with his support (in which refusal you are, no doubt, perfectly right), he must be placed in the charge of the parish authorities. I am one of the parish authorities myself," he continued, with the same peculiar smile, which often recurred to Hester Rowe's mind and puzzled her in days to come, " and I shall be happy to take charge of him for the present."

Mrs. Rowe made no objection to the proposal. Bertie's little cap was found for him : he had no other possession except his one broken toy ; and he was lifted to the back seat beside the groom. Mrs. Rowe bade him no farewell. He put up his mouth for a kiss, but she turned away from him. Some grain of conscience told her that she was acting towards a worse than orphaned child with cruel harshness, for faults that were not its own. Mr. Hervey waited only to say a word of warning in her ear.

"Mind, Mrs. Rowe, if you mention Mr. Ravenscroft's name in connection with this child, you'll get into trouble. You know nothing, and your suspicions are libellous."

"Libellous or not, sir," said Mrs. Rowe coolly, " they are true."

Mr. Hervey shrugged his shoulders and departed. He took the reins from his groom, and drove towards Mickleham. But after driving for a mile or two upon the road, he turned back and made his way to his own house. He was a man who generally indulged his whims and fancies; and a certain fancy had taken possession of him now. Little Bertram did not see the inside of Mickleham Workhouse that afternoon.

Of course Gaston had never received Mrs. Rowe's letter. It had fallen into the hands of Madame Waldstein before his return from Wiesbaden; and she, learning from what quarter it had come, took to herself the right of opening it and of consulting Mr. Hervey as to the answer that should be returned to Hester Rowe. "Gaston would find it very awkward," she said, "as he will probably now reside in this neighbourhood, if the Rowes made this statement public. Go and see, Richard, whether you cannot silence them and get the unlucky child sent to a workhouse or an orphanage or something. I *know* that Gaston only wants to have the tribe off his hands. They have all been begging of him for the last four or five years. I am glad that the girl is dead at last."

"Gaston has behaved very unhandsomely to her," said Richard Hervey in a tone of disgust.

"Abominably," said Madame Waldstein. She was a handsome woman still in spite of her sixty-three years and her half-crippled state: she sat up erect as she spoke, with a wonderful brightness in her quick dark eyes. She had been greatly overcome by the news of Philip's death, but she was so far herself by this time as to be able to make arrangements for the future of her second son. "I want him to marry," she remarked. "He can make a fresh beginning now that Lucy Moore is out of the way."

"This letter is not your first intimation then of his connection with her?"

"Certainly not," said the old lady briskly. "I have known the whole story more or less ever since she left Netherby with Gaston. But, as he did not trouble me about it, I never said a word to him. It was no business of mine, and if I had opposed it, he might have put a seal upon his folly by marrying her out of sheer obstinacy. Now they are separated for ever, and nobody can imagine that I contrived their separation or even counted upon it."

"You did contrive it then, Leonora?"

Madame Waldstein laughed. "Do not ask too many questions," she said significantly. "The matter is ended now. And, for heaven's sake, do not mention it to Gaston. I will speak to him."

Mr. Hervey's curiosity was aroused by this interview. He had no great liking for his cousin, Madame Waldstein, and would not have been sorry to do her an ill turn; but he agreed with her in thinking it right that Gaston should be separated from the Rowes, and that the child should not be brought up in a place where every one would comment upon his history and his parentage. Madame Waldstein went on to make a proposition that a cheap school should be found where the boy might be boarded for a time and taught a trade: she herself would furnish the money for that purpose and make the Rowes a handsome present for their future silence. But when Mr. Hervey visited the cottage he found that no bribes were necessary. Hester Rowe was neither disposed to keep the child nor to talk about him in the village. She was only anxious to get rid of him; and Mr. Hervey was accordingly enabled to drive off in triumph, with the avowed intention of placing the boy in Mickleham Workhouse.

Madame Waldstein had her own ends to serve

in what she was doing, and she served them well. She said that she knew the whole story of Gaston and Lucy Moore; if so, she concealed part of her knowledge very skilfully. Never by look or word did she let any one suspect (or show that she suspected) that Lucy had been Gaston's wife. It would not have suited her plans at all that little Bertram Ravenscroft should be brought home and acknowledged as Gaston's son and heir.

As soon as Felicia was safely housed at Ravenscroft Hall, Gaston's fruitless expedition to Elmstone took place—an expedition upon which he set off so precipitately that his mother had not time to intercept him and to make the communication to him which she was anxious that he should receive as soon as possible. Gaston, however, returned to Netherby with great speed : he thought it likely that Lucy had gone to her friends, the Rowes. He was very angry with her for acting so foolishly, but he was also prepared to forgive her, and to tell her that her troubles now were over—that all the world should know that she had been his wife for the last four years and more. But when he reached the Rowes' cottage, he found it deserted. It should be mentioned that Hester was in the habit of going away sometimes for long tramps over the lanes and fields—tramps which often extended through a period of days and weeks: it was one of the ways in which her gipsy origin showed itself; and she had quitted Netherby for that purpose soon after Mr. Hervey took Bertie away with him. The cottage door was locked, the windows were closely shuttered; not a sign of life was to be seen. Clearly Lucy could not be there.

Gaston, dismayed and aggrieved, scarcely knew what his next steps ought to be. After some anxious thought he determined to go to Mr. Hervey, lay the facts of the case before him, and ask him for his advice. He was resolved that as soon as Lucy was found, all secrecy should be at once and for ever at an end. His first step in this direction should be an acknowledgment of the truth to his cousin, Richard Hervey, for whom Gaston had a sort of respect if not much affection.

But disappointment followed upon disappointment. Mr. Hervey had suddenly shut up his house and gone abroad. Gaston asked in some surprise whither he had gone, and was told that Mr. Hervey intended to spend the coming winter in the south of France. The young man turned away, and retraced his steps to his own home, intending to see his mother and explain the matter to her. If he could not find Lucy at once, he must spend all his time and energy in the search for her until he was successful. Madame Waldstein should know the state of affairs at once.

He presented himself in his mother's room with a troubled and downcast air which told her his errand before he spoke. The last few days of sorrow and anxiety were beginning to tell upon him : his eyes were haggard and his hands shook. Madame Waldstein looked at him searchingly, and raised her forefinger.

"Wait!" she said sharply. "I have something to tell you before you begin to speak. I know what you are here for ; you wish to tell me about Lucy Moore."

Gaston stared at her in dumb bewilderment. "How do you know?" he stammered after a pause.

"I always know anything that I choose to

know. She left Elmstone on the day after the one on which you started for Wiesbaden, and she came to Netherby. She was ill and over-fatigued, I suppose: she reached Hester Rowe's cottage in a fainting state——"

Gaston rose to his feet. "Where is she?" he said, his eyes blazing with excitement. "You know where she is—let me go to her——"

"My poor Gaston," said his mother quietly, "control yourself. You have bad news to hear. Sit down and take it quietly."

"Is she ill?" he questioned. "Dangerously ill? For God's sake, mother, speak. Don't you know how I love her?"

Madame Waldstein looked at him curiously. His voice was broken with emotion; his face was gray. She began to fear the effect of her communication; but she could not retract her words. She must go on.

"She *was* ill," she said with a reluctance which looked like sympathy. "For three days she was very ill. Then she succumbed—it had been too much for her strength. On the third day—she died—of fever."

Gaston reeled as if from a sudden blow.

"And the child?" he said hoarsely. "The child is here—with you?——"

"The child?" said his mother, avoiding his gaze as she made the statement which she knew so well he would misunderstand: "her child was buried with her. He died the day after the mother——"

She said no more. Gaston had fallen and lay like a dead man at her feet. The blow had been too heavy a one for him to bear—wife and child taken from him at a stroke. It was perhaps a merciful thing that a severe illness rendered him unconscious of his loss for many days and weeks. But the slow return to health and strength was a terrible time for Gaston Ravenscroft.

His mother was astonished to find him contented with so little explanation. During his convalescence he asked only a few questions concerning the way in which these matters had come to her ears, and on this point she found it easy to satisfy him. She brought the clergyman who had read the funeral service over Lucy's grave and the doctor who had attended her, cautioning both beforehand to say nothing about the child, "as poor Gaston could not bear to hear him mentioned," in order to answer any questions that he might wish to ask; but he asked none. He was so silent and depressed that his friends feared for his sanity, and it was with great unwillingness that they heard him at last announce his intention of leaving Netherby for London. He did not say what he meant to do in London; but Madame Waldstein hazarded a shrewd guess when she said, with a significant nod of her handsome old head—

"London! He will not stay long in London! He is bound for Elmstone to see his fool's paradise again. And I hope that he may come back to us safe and sound!"

Thus the first act of Gaston Ravenscroft's life was played, and he was sorely inclined to wish that it had been the last.

PART II.—VERA.

CHAPTER V.

ON THE ELMSTONE DOWNS.

MADAME WALDSTEIN was right. Gaston had gone once more to Elmstone.

It was now the month of August. The sun blazed hotly in a cloudless heaven. The sea was blue as the sky itself, and the wind-swept downs were rich with golden gorse and purple heather, over which the great brown bees went humming and the butterflies hovered on the wing. The grass was scanty and yellow; it had been withered by a month of drought. The ground was cracked and burnt; the birds were silent; there was nowhere any life, any motion, any sound. Far away on the one hand lay the shining sea, its blue unflecked by even a single cloudlike sail.

The summer silence seemed more dreary—at least to one or two persons on the Elmstone downs that day—than a tempest of wintry rain and wind could have done.

Gaston Ravenscroft was not so much alone as he imagined himself to be when he flung himself down that day upon the scorched bare earth and thought of all that he had lost. Life had grown unendurable: in the madness of his grief he fancied himself justified in putting an end to it. He had the remedy for his woes at hand: why should it not be used? But between him and that desperate remedy a barrier was about to be interposed—a barrier of which he did not as yet suspect the existence. His safeguard was near him, though he knew it not, in the shape of a little child.

This child—a little girl of nine or ten years of age—had been wandering over the downs for two or three hours, and had finally seated herself in the shadow of a lichen-covered boulder in order to cry over her own troubles, which were as real and perhaps as great to her as those of Gaston Ravenscroft were to him. She was a pale, neglected-looking little creature, with wild, strange gray eyes, which looked odd beneath her long black eyelashes and dark brows, and a wealth of very fair hair. Her frock was torn and shabby, and she crouched down beneath the sheltering stone in an attitude of fear or pain, sobbing loudly and passionately from time to time and again holding her breath as if afraid to make another sound.

It was long before the stillness of her refuge quieted the weeping child. The chirping of a grasshopper at last attracted her attention : she forgot her grief a little in watching the movements of his quaint green body and slender legs. When he had leaped out of her sight she looked round, with tears still glazing her fevered cheeks, and became suddenly aware of her own loneliness. It frightened her a little. She rose and moved out of the shadow of the boulder into the glare of the sun and stared nervously about her : there was nothing in the guise of a human creature but herself to be seen between earth and sky.

She walked on dreamily ; her footsteps made no sound upon the heather. She scarcely even frightened the rabbits until she was close upon

them. In spite of her troubles, her languor, her
sense of loneliness, she laughed to see the way
in which they kicked up their heels and scurried
off as she drew near—their white scuts betray-
ing them before they whisked into the darkness
of their burrows. She stood to watch a furry
mother with a group of little ones around her.
A sound of running water reached her ears:
there was a fissure in the limestone rock beneath
her, and at the bottom of it a streamlet tinkled
musically. She looked and watched; perhaps
she moved, for the rabbit family disappeared at
lightning speed; or perhaps it was something
else that moved, not far away. The child turned
her head with a spasm of visible fear. But all
that she saw was a man lying face downwards
upon the shrivelled grass.

She thought of flying; then changed her
mind. The man did not move: he was probably
asleep. Even if he were awake, she reflected,
he was not likely to do her any harm. She was
not afraid of strangers: they were often kinder
to her than the people with whom she dwelt.
She would not disturb him by a sound, although
he lay straight across her path—a narrow sheep-

track which she was following out of very idleness;—she would make a circuit and pursue her
way.   But first, moved by what instinct she
knew not, she surveyed the stranger's motionless
figure with profound interest.

It was no man with whom she was acquainted.
It was not Mr. Stanger, her step-father, whose
black coat—grown shiny at the shoulders—
always reminded her irresistibly of a blackbeetle;
nor was it "old Davy," as she called him, although he was not really old, but only bent with
the weight of sorrow and of toil—the musician
of Mr. Stanger's troupe, lame and undersized,
and clad in garments that were rusty with age
and soiled and frayed to the last degree of
shabbiness.   This man was neither small nor
badly dressed nor apparently old; his frame was
strongly made; his hat was thrown aside and
displayed a head covered with short black locks
—not a gray hair amongst them.

Was he asleep indeed? the child asked herself; and one glance at his attitude sufficed as a
reply to the question.   His face was hidden on
his left arm; the other was flung wide, and the
right hand clutched the earth convulsively.   The

thin white fingers were clenched : the nails were digging into the baked earth. From time to time a shudder passed through all his limbs : once he even uttered a faint groan or gasp—but only once. His agony was not to be lightened by words or sighs : he was about to choose a speedier method of relief.

The child stood transfixed by this spectacle of sorrow such as she had never known,—wondering whether he suffered bodily pain, whether she ought to speak to him, or go to the nearest cottage for help. Suddenly his attitude changed. The grasp of the hand relaxed : he drew his arm slowly towards him. The nails were livid with the force which he had used. Then he was still. He seemed to be searching his pockets—was it for food, medicine, brandy? the child wondered to herself. She watched and waited with prudence and self-command beyond her years.

He raised himself a little on his elbow and glanced around. She thought that he had seen her, but she dared not move. The event proved her wrong. Gaston Ravenscroft's weary, bloodshot eyes failed to distinguish her little brown figure from the dried earth and the stones. He thought himself quite alone—with nothing near him but those terrible blank spaces of sky and sea and barren land.

What was it that his fingers held ? A little thing, not larger than a toy, something made of rosewood and polished metal that glittered brightly in the sunshine. He raised his hand. Rashly and wickedly enough he had made up his mind that the earth would be well quit of Gaston Ravenscroft.

But before he had pulled the trigger, the child had leapt forward with a sharp, frightened cry. She understood the gesture well enough—understood it as scarcely one child of her age in a hundred would have done. For she belonged to a company of players: a strolling troupe devoted to melodrama on the boards of provincial theatres; and her experience of sensational plays and players interpreted to her that little movement of the hand. She cried out loudly and passionately and bade him stop.

Gaston Ravenscroft lowered his hand and started violently. Then he raised himself into a sitting posture, and looked at the unfamiliar little figure with haggard eyes. She stood before

him trembling with excitement, and holding out
her hands.

"Oh, don't!" she said. "Don't go on.
Don't you know how wicked it is? *Please*
don't do that."

He looked at her with a sort of dull wonder-
ment and then dropped his face upon his hands.
The beads of perspiration stood upon his forehead. A minute ago and she had trembled. It
was his turn to tremble now. He shook like an
aspen leaf, and began to breathe heavily.

The child, with her old-fashioned, thin little
face still quivering, drew near and touched him
on the shoulder. "Are you ill?" she said
anxiously. "Can I do anything for you?"

"No, nothing. Go away."

She retreated for a few steps, but she did not go.
Her eyes were fixed upon the revolver, which was
now lying upon the ground. It seemed to have
a fascination for her: she could not lift her eyes
from it.

In a short time Gaston made an effort for
composure. He let one hand fall to his side,
but kept the other over his pale face as he
said :

"Why do you not go?   Do you want money? Take it."   He threw a piece of silver at her feet.

"I don't want your money," she answered sullenly.   "I only want to be sure that—that you won't try to hurt yourself."

"What if I did?" muttered Gaston to himself with a short laugh.   Then he lifted his head and looked at her.   "Who are you?" he said. "What are you doing here?   You startled me; you might have caused an accident."

"But it would not have been an accident," she said, looking back at him in a grave and un-child-like manner.   "You were doing it on purpose.   I have seen people act in that way at the theatre.   But you were in earnest."

"In earnest?" he echoed bitterly.   "Well— I don't know—perhaps I was——"

He had forgotten her presence.   His dark miserable face was turned towards the sea.   The child's opportunity had come.   She made a desperate effort over her fears,—for she had a secret dread of all firearms,—picked up the revolver, which he seemed to have forgotten, and suddenly dropped it down the fissure in the cliff, where she had listened to the running water not long before. She heard it strike the limestone rock in its descent. Then she burst into an agony of tears.

Gaston made an angry movement towards her, but stopped short as soon as she began to sob. His eyes had already begun to look less wild and strained; as he observed the little figure for a moment or two in silence his face assumed a more natural hue and expression. When he spoke again it was with curious calmness.

"What made you do that? How do you suppose I shall get it back again?"

"You won't get it back!" cried the small girl, stamping on the ground with a mixture of passion and triumph, which absolutely silenced him. "You will never see it again. That crack is so deep that nobody can climb down it, and there is water at the bottom. Why should you want to get it back? Did you never think how dreadful it would be to lie here all alone, and nobody to find you for days and days?"

"You are a very odd child!" said Gaston slowly. Then he rose and walked up and down for a few paces, with his eyes bent upon the ground. In a short time he came back to her and spoke.

"Do you understand," he said, "that you are not to chatter to anybody about what you have seen and heard to-day?"

She raised her eyes to his and stood silent.

"You are not to say that you saw me here: you are not to mention the revolver—do you hear? If you do, I shall find means to punish you; understand that. If you will hold your tongue, I will make it worth your while; I will give you a present—anything you like. I won't have my affairs gossiped about."

Still she did not answer. He frowned and looked annoyed.

"How much do you want?" he said. "A sovereign? Here, take it. Don't you understand me?"

"I understand quite well," the child answered in a low voice. "But there's no need for you to give me anything. I won't take it. I shall not say a word about you."

"Not even at your own home, remember."

"I have no home."

"No home? What do you mean? Where are you going?" said Gaston, in a tone of extreme irritation.

"I don't know. I don't care. I have run away."

He looked at her intently. Little by little his brow cleared; in a few minutes he laughed aloud.

"Better and better. We are in like case— waifs and strays, trying to escape from the burdens Fate lays upon us. What are *you* running away from? Is it my duty to take you back to your friends, I wonder?"

"If you do," the child cried passionately, "I'll tell everybody everything about you."

He laughed contemptuously. "Tell what you like. I have changed my mind about it. What is your name?"

"Vera Marlitt," she answered with some reluctance. Gaston's face suddenly changed.

"What name?" he said.

She repeated it, and he looked at her with a long keen gaze of inquiry.

"Come here," he said presently in a gentler tone. "Don't be afraid of me; I won't take you back against your will; but I should like to hear a little more about you. Let us sit down somewhere; it is very hot, and I am tired."

He led the way to one of the great boulders which were to be found at intervals about the downs, and stretched himself upon the turf with his back to the stone. The little girl followed him slowly; child as she was, she was surprised to see him draw out a cigar-case. "If I am not to shuffle off this mortal coil just yet, I may as well refresh myself with a cigar," he said with would-be carelessness. "Do you object, Mademoiselle?"

"You may smoke if you like. My name is Vera," she replied with dignity. "Nobody calls me Mademoiselle."

"But I shall call you Mademoiselle if I choose. It is a privilege reserved for me alone. What have I here?" and he suddenly pulled out of his pocket a little tin case. "Oh, sandwiches! What an anti-climax! Franklyn must have put them up; they are of no use to me."

Thus speaking, he flung the case to some little distance; then turned again to Vera. "What, crying once more! What is the matter now?"

"I'm very sorry," said the child, submissively trying to restrain her tears. "It's only that I am tired and—hungry."

She had enough pride to make this confession a difficult one. But the throwing away of the sandwich-box had upset all her self-control.

He gave her a curious look; one in which surprise mingled with a sort of pity. Then he rose, marched to the spot where the tin case had alighted, picked it up and deposited it in her lap.

"I beg your pardon, child," he said, more gently than he had spoken yet. "I was thoughtless. But a good deal ought to be forgiven to a man in my circumstances. By the by, I suppose that some people would say that you had saved my life; I owe you thanks for taking the trouble, though I own I think it was thrown away. Eat the sandwiches, my dear; I assure you that Franklyn prepares them excellently."

He leaned against the stone, with the cigar in his mouth, and closed his eyes. The nonchalance of his attitude amazed the child; she was not old enough to read the signs of pain and trouble in the dark shadows beneath his eyes, the pale mouth, the bent brow, and twitching fingers. She could not tell that she saw before her a man who was feeling the exhaustion consequent on a prolonged mental strain, or one whose nerves had been thoroughly shaken by grief and illness. She meditated silently upon the carelessness of his demeanour, as she ate the sandwiches which he had given to her. It was not until she had consumed the last mouthful that he roused himself and looked at her with a faint curious smile.

CHAPTER VI.

A NEW PURPOSE.

" WELL," said Gaston, turning his face towards
the child, as she finished the last mouthful, " I
want to hear something more of you. Surely a
waif and stray like myself can look after a waif
and stray like you. Don't you think so ?"

The wearily ironical tone perplexed the child.
Seeing this, he flung away his cigar, glanced at
her again, and said seriously :

" Tell me your name once more."

" Vera Marlitt. They call me Vera de
Lusignan at the theatre."

" Why do they call you so ?" said Gaston,
whose eyes began to glow with curious brightness as he listened to her.

" Because I was born in France at a place
called Lusignan, and my mother said it would

make a good stage-name for me when I began to sing.   I think Mr. Stanger told her to say so."

"And who is Mr. Stanger?"

"The manager.   I hate him."

"Is he a relation of yours?"

"No.   I haven't any relations."

"But your mother and father——" Gaston began, with increasing interest.

"They are dead."

"Dead? ah, yes.   But your father—what was his name?"

"His name was Ernst Marlitt.   He was a German—a musician," said the little girl, with serious eyes.   "He died in France when I was a very little girl; and mamma and I were left alone.   Mamma was an Englishwoman.   When my father died she had to work very hard, and she was so ill that she said she would come back to England, and see whether anybody would help us there.   I don't think anybody helped us.   We met the Stangers; and Mr. Stanger got mamma to play the piano during his entertainments and to act sometimes, and by and by she married him."

"Child, do you know your mother's name before she married your father?"

"Yes," said little Vera. "It was Hervey."

"I thought so," Gaston murmured to himself. "This is an odd coincidence indeed. Go on, Vera. Why did she marry Stanger?"

"She said she did it for my sake," said Vera, drawing a deep breath. "I don't know why. Perhaps she was afraid to say no. And then Mr. Stanger brought me out as the Infant Prodigy. But mamma died a few months afterwards, and I was left to Mr. Stanger."

"Who takes care of you? Has he married again?"

"No. I don't want any one to take care of me. There are the Miss Stangers, his grown-up daughters; they manage everything."

"Are they kind to you?"

"No."

"No? Why not?"

Vera spoke sullenly and decisively. "They hate me. They hated my mother. They call me the little Dutch doll. They pinch me and box my ears when nobody sees them. But I should not mind them so much if—if——"

"If what? This is quite a case of Cinderella and her cruel sisters! Well, if what?"

"If Mr. Stanger did not beat me!" she answered, with an irrepressible sob, and overflow of tears.

He did not speak for a moment, and then he muttered a word or two below his breath.

"What brutes!" Vera heard him say. As she continued to sob, he put out his hand and gently stroked her bare ruffled head. There was almost a wistful tenderness in his tone when he spoke again.

"Poor little thing! Poor little neglected Cinderella!" Then after another pause:

"Was that why you ran away?"

For answer the child pulled up the loose sleeve of her shabby brown frock, and showed some livid marks upon her arm. "He did that this morning, and more than that, because I did not sing well enough to please him. I was hoarse and couldn't get up to the high notes. And I didn't know the steps of a new dance very well. He said it was all sham and obstinacy, and that he would flog it out of me once for all. But he broke the little cane that he generally uses, you know, and he went out to fetch his riding-whip,—he said he would make me dance to another tune,—and while he was gone, Davy the fiddler helped me to get out of the window, and I ran away. You won’t take me back to him, will you? He would kill me, I know he would.”

Gaston was biting his long dark moustache savagely; his eyes glowed with a new fire. But his answer was very gently spoken.

“ I will see that you come to no harm, little Vera. I shall not let this business go on at any rate. I have a right to interfere.”

He fell to meditating. She did not understand him, but she dried her tears, feeling a childlike trust in his ability and willingness to save her from all present and future annoyances. Presently he spoke :

“Vera, would you like to go to school ?”

“ I don’t know,” she said doubtfully. “ Emily Stanger says that everybody will always laugh at me. I should not like a whole school to laugh at me.”

“ Why should they laugh ?”

Little Vera’s face grew crimson. “ I am poor, for one thing—and ugly—and stupid,” she stammered.

“ I shouldn’t have thought you stupid. As

for poverty, nobody but fools would laugh at you for that."

Vera said nothing, but she twisted a corner of her apron and regarded him wistfully. She did not dare to ask the question that was in her mind, Was she indeed so very ugly? That she was hideously plain had been instilled into her mind with jibes and sneers from her earliest days in Mr. Stanger's household. Had not Emily Stanger that very morning boxed her ears for no other reason than that she was, as Miss Stanger said, "such a mean-looking little toad!" And indeed she was small and slight, even to leanness; her skin was colourless; her hair, which under a mother's care might have proved a redeeming feature, was lustreless and tangled. Only when she sang in a more important part than usual was any notice taken of her dress; and then she was encouraged in a love for finery rather than for neatness.

Vera's companion looked at her oddly, then laughed in his sarcastic way. "Daughter of Eve," he said, "I know what you are thinking of. I'll leave other people to talk to you about your looks, little one."

Vera bit her lip; the colour rushed to her cheeks and the tears to her eyes. She turned away to hide her face, but in vain. Gaston's keen gaze followed her; his face wore an amused expression, tempered with pity, which she could not at all understand. For the moment she was unmixedly miserable.

"You little fool!" said Gaston, not unkindly, at last. His voice had quite recovered the musical ring which was its peculiar characteristic. "I should not have thought you so full of vanity! So you want compliments to your pretty eyes already, do you? Silly child! you will hear plenty of them in half a dozen years or so!"

"Do you really mean it?" said Vera, wiping away her tears. "But I don't believe it; you are kinder than other people—that is all. I don't mind what they say—much."

"Don't you? And you won't mind going back to them, I suppose?"

"Back to Mr. Stanger? Oh, won't you— won't you—take me away with *you?*"

"That might be difficult, little one."

"I *won't* go back to Mr. Stanger," was the child's response.

He frowned a little, eyed her with that keen gaze which seemed to penetrate the inmost recesses of her heart, and then bestirred himself to speak seriously.

"You have been badly treated," he said, "and I should like to help you to get away from these people; but I can do nothing if you are going to behave like a foolish child. You seem to have sense and spirit beyond your age: use them and listen to me. If that man thinks he has lost you, he will advertise and search the country—because you must be a valuable possession to him—and you might be given back to him and treated worse than before without hope of redress. If you walk quietly back with me, *I* will arrange matters with him." There was a world of haughty meaning in the emphasis that he laid upon the pronoun. "*I* shall not stand by and let him abuse you. But you will have to confront him, perhaps, and stick to your story—I think you are brave enough for that? You do not seem to want for courage. If you will do this I will help you."

Vera looked up with a glow of confidence and pride. "I'll do *anything* for you," she said, childishly enough. But her emotion of reverence and admiration for her new friend and benefactor was anything but childish.

"That is well," he said gravely; and with these words she was content.

Meanwhile a slight change had come over the scene around them. A rising breeze had driven some light fleecy clouds between the earth and the sun, which mitigated the fierceness of the heat: the shadows were less strongly marked: the birds chirped and flew low as if they thought the evening hours approached. Gaston looked at his watch and suddenly rose to his feet.

"It is not so hot now," he said. "How far are we from the town?"

"I do not know."

"Two miles only," he went on reflectively. "I suppose that you can walk two miles, Vera?"

"Yes."

He looked round him silently. For a few moments he totally forgot the child's presence: a sad and dreamy expression stole into his eyes. At last he sighed deeply, passed his hand over his forehead, then turned to Vera.

"So we must go and take up our burdens once

more, must we, little one?" he said, with an indescribable sweetness of intonation in which, child as she was, she could distinguish a note of profound melancholy. "I had a wild dream of escaping from mine—like yourself, you see—and in counselling you to be brave, I have brought myself to reason. I must put off the day of escape a little longer—if only for your sake, Vera. Shall we go back together?"

He held out his hand. She placed her hot little fingers within his strong but gentle clasp, and they turned their faces to the town.

Scarcely a word was spoken during that two miles' walk. It was well for Vera that she was accustomed to much active exercise,—she escaped from the Stangers for a country ramble as often as she was able,—for her companion walked fast and took little notice of her. Only when they neared the town did he slacken his pace at all.

"You must come with me to the 'Falcon,' Vera," he said curtly. "I will see Stanger alone."

And, holding her still by the hand, he turned towards the inn where he had been staying since the previous evening. Here he summoned a servant who had come with him from Netherby and consigned Vera to his care. He had business in the town, he said, and Franklyn must see that the young lady was made comfortable and happy whilst he was away.

Vera was accordingly given into the hands of a friendly chambermaid, who washed her face and brushed her hair, and then she was provided with a good dinner, of which she certainly stood in need. When this was over she curled herself up in a corner of the sofa, and there, overpowered by fatigue and soothed by the quietness of the place, fell fast asleep and did not wake until late in the afternoon. Even then she was aroused only by the sound of voices close beside her ; and, starting up, she found herself confronted by the faces of the two men, each of whom wished to establish a right to her guardianship. Mr. Ravenscroft had returned in company with Mr. Jonas Stanger.

Mr. Stanger's manner was exceedingly obsequious, but his face wore a viciously disappointed look. Mr. Ravenscroft's haughty features showed an admixture of anger and contempt.

" I brought her up as my own child," Mr. Stanger was observing in an oily whine. " I treated her as a father. And is this the return she

makes me?   Alas! child of my lost, my sainted
Mabel! why do you malign me thus?"   This
last ejaculation was accompanied with a well-
managed sob and flourish of his handkerchief.

"Are you awake, Vera?" said Mr. Ravenscroft.   "Come here to me.   Show me your arm
again.   There is the lie to your professions of
affection, Mr. Stanger.   Don't you think you
had better hold your tongue?"

"Did she dare to insinuate that I ill-treated
her?" said the manager, casting a venomous
glance at her bruised arm and shrinking figure.
"It was an accident—a fall."

"I have heard your story already," said Vera's
friend contemptuously.   "You know exactly how
much confidence I place in it.   Vera, listen to
me.   This man agrees to set you free—to hand
you over to me, in fact—on certain conditions,
which I need not specify; but," he added, drawing her out of Mr. Stanger's hearing and speaking
low, "he will not consent, on any terms, to your
not singing at the theatre to-night.   I can
guarantee his not ill-treating you during that
time; it would be against his own interest to do
so, the cur.   I have unfortunately no *right* to

interfere exactly; the person who has a right is now away from England, and he knows that; therefore he refuses to yield more than absolute fear requires him to do. However, I'll explain all that to you another time. Will you do what he wishes, child? In another day you will be free."

"He looks as if he would kill me!" Vera murmured doubtfully.

"He dare not lay a finger on you, child. Don't be afraid. You can stay here till the evening; I will have you taken to the theatre and brought safely home at night."

"And you will come to the theatre too? I will sing if you are there, but I shall be afraid of him if you are away."

A look of repugnance came over Gaston's face. He had been to that theatre once before— with Lucy. But in view of the child's evident terror he could not refuse to accompany her.

"Then I will go," she said readily enough, "and I will sing my best, my very best, because you will be there."

He turned back to Mr. Stanger and gave him the reply that the manager was awaiting.

"She will sing for you once more; you know on what conditions. There need be no rehearsal, I suppose? I will send some one with her to-night, and I shall be in the theatre myself to take her away after the performance. Remember that she is my property now, not yours."

"I am sure, sir," said Mr. Stanger with servile humility, "if I had known that she had friends so able and willing to serve her I——"

"You would have treated her with civility? I have no doubt of it," said the young man dryly. And Mr. Stanger took his leave in some confusion.

Vera was still too much of a child to wonder at Mr. Ravenscroft's kindness to her. If she had been nothing but the waif and stray which she appeared it is probable that he would merely have made her a present and perhaps remonstrated with the manager concerning his treatment of her, but he would never once have thought of rescuing her from an unhappy life or of taking any responsibility upon himself concerning her. But the utterance of her name had at once arrested his attention. Marlitt? It was a man of the name of Marlitt who had persuaded Mabel Hervey to run away with him. Gaston well remembered the enthusiastic musician, with his long hair and visionary eyes, in the days when he lived at Mickleham and came to Netherby Manor to instruct Miss Hervey in violin-playing, in harmony, and counterpoint. Mabel Hervey had a passion for the violin, and was not wanting in genuine musical talent. The lessons ended, however, in her running away with Ernst Marlitt and marrying him. Gaston was present when the announcement of the marriage was made to Mr. Hervey, and well remembered the old man's burst of anger and grief. Since that time little news of Mabel had come to Netherby, but Gaston had certainly heard of the birth of a child (a little girl with a Russian name—he had forgotten whether it was Olga, Vera, or Nadia, but he knew that it was Russian), also of Ernst Marlitt's death and Mabel's subsequent marriage with a theatrical manager, whose name he did not know.

Thus placed on the track, he followed it up with ease. Mr. Stanger placed in his hands all the papers belonging to Mabel which had come into his possession, and agreed to deliver Vera over to him in return for the payment of a sum of money. Gaston did not as yet know what he should do with the child. He would write of course to Richard Hervey to tell him of his little granddaughter's position, and no doubt, he thought, Hervey would decide what should become of her. If he refused to give her a home Gaston thought it probable that his mother and sister-in-law would find a place for Vera at Ravenscroft Hall. She would be a nice playmate for little Olivia, and the second cousins could share the same advantages.

Had he been in a more genial mood he would have told Vera of his relationship to her. But he wanted energy to do it. Felicia would make the communication better than he. And perhaps it would be as well to wait until it was seen how Mr. Hervey took the news, and what he meant to do for his granddaughter.

CHAPTER VII.

DAVY'S PUPIL.

At nine o'clock that evening Vera was seated in a little room behind the scenes of the Elmstone theatre, dressed in a very short and flimsy costume, her face plastered with paint and powder, her hair crowned with gaudy artificial flowers. Mr. Ravenscroft had taken care that she should be well guarded. Mrs. Kemp herself, the landlady of the "Falcon," had been persuaded to accompany Vera "behind the scenes" —an office of which she did not altogether approve, as she considered it rather beneath her dignity. But it had been represented to her by Mr. Ravenscroft's confidential servant, whom he had brought from Netherby, that without some protector the little girl would probably be "pinched, nipped, and bobbed" between the acts, and kidnapped by Mr. Stanger afterwards; and this picture had produced the desired result of bringing Mrs. Kemp to the theatre in Vera's company.

Upright and severe in her respectable bonnet and shawl, Mrs. Kemp sat in the dressing-room, her comely face expressive of some interest, but of more dislike, of her surroundings. Two or three girls ran in and out; a demon in black and red stood at the door smoking a cigar. Miss Julia Stanger was touching up her eyebrows before the glass and withering Vera by her sarcasms. Vera had not had a flattering reception. Miss Emily Stanger had gone into hysterics upon her appearance, and expressed a wish to tear "the German toad's eyes out;" Julia had been prevented from boxing the child's ears only by a rough admonition from her father; the rest of the company had had hints or orders not to treat her with friendliness. But, now that Mr. Stanger was out of the way, Julia's tongue ran on unchecked by Mrs. Kemp's austere presence.

"I wonder you can look any of us in the face, miss!" said the fair Julia indignantly. "Telling lies about my pa in the way you have done! You'll say Emily and me were unkind to you next, which we weren't, you little viper!"

"Yes, you were," said Vera, who was in no patient mood.

"If giving you the best to eat and to drink, and taking you about with us to the first hotels, and treating you like a lady instead of the beggar's brat that you are—if *that's* unkindness, then we were unkind; and I should like to know what next!" said Julia fluently. "And now you turn on us, you little wretch! I wouldn't have such a bad disposition, oh, not for worlds! would you, Miss Spratt?"

"Oh, not for worlds!" said Miss Spratt, a thin girl with a pursed-up mouth and watery blue eyes, whom Vera hated almost as much as she hated the two Miss Stangers.

"Don't you go for to answer them, dear," said Mrs. Kemp in an undertone. "They ain't worth it, the impudent hussies!"

It was fortunate for her that this speech was unheard by the two girls, or there would have been a disturbance. It produced no calming effect upon Vera's own mind. She was intoxicated by the prospect of freedom, and not disposed to leave Miss Stanger's abuse unanswered.

"You have always been unkind to me," she said. "You often kept me without food when I was hungry; you often pinched and pushed me when I was on the stage, so that I might forget my part and be punished; you often made your father beat me. I have not told Mr. Ravenscroft all about you yet, but I shall—I shall tell him what a bad, wicked, cruel girl you are; and when you are acting in different towns, he will tell people about you, and they will come and hiss."

It was a childish speech, but Julia had been known to fly into a fury for less. On this occasion, however, she made an obvious effort to govern herself.

"You little story-teller!" she said contemptuously. "What do I care for your Ravenscroft? He's none so grand, if the truth were told, nor so saintly either. As for *you*, everybody knows where *you* came from; your mother was a beggar or worse, and your father a rogue and a vagabond—that's about the truth of it."

"My father was a gentleman," said Vera,

rising to her feet, and looking at her with eyes before which she quailed in spite of herself; "and my mother was a lady, and your father killed her with being so cruel both to her and to me. You think you can torment me as you like, because there is nobody to take care of me. Did you never hear that God curses the people who are cruel to the poor and fatherless, Julia Stanger? You will have to ask Him to forgive you for your behaviour to me before ever you hope to go to heaven."

Vera's speech was certainly indefensible. It was the outcome of the state of excitement in which she had spent the day. Besides, she had had a theatrical training. She was partly quoting from a play that she had once seen acted; nevertheless, she was terribly in earnest, and her earnestness told upon the hearers. Mrs. Kemp made a clicking sound of disapprobation; Miss Spratt uttered a scream, and ran out of the room; Julia turned pale beneath her rouge. But in an instant Miss Stanger recovered herself. The blood rushed to her bold handsome face; she struck the child furiously on the head with the back of a hair-brush, and would certainly have repeated the blow but for the vigorous interposition of Mrs. Kemp. At that very moment came Vera's call; she left Mrs. Kemp to settle the matter with Julia as best she could, and made her appearance on the stage.

She had little acting to do, but she had two songs—one a comic " patter " song, and one of a more pathetic character. Vera was never nervous when singing, and she gave forth her comic utterances and performed the accompanying dance with more spirit than usual after the encounter with Julia. She was applauded to the echo ; but it was not until the close of the second repetition of the last verse—a very slangy one, the meaning of which she scarcely understood—that she caught sight of Mr. Ravenscroft, looking as if he did anything but enjoy the performance. He was sitting far back in one of the boxes : his arms crossed, a dark frown upon his brow. Vera was disappointed. She had hoped to please him by her singing, and she went off with tears in her eyes.

The interval between the two songs was not great, and she had to change her dress in the meantime. Her exultation had been followed by sudden shame and depression : an intense realisation of her own loneliness came upon her as she stole back, in picturesque rags and poverty, to the darkened stage, and sang as if she were telling her own story to the world.   How came the Stangers to give the child so suitable a part ? Even to Vera's own ears her voice rang out with a passionate thrill of real emotion as she sang.

The last verse ran as follows :—

" My heart it is sore, and the cold wind is driving,
    In the grave with my mother I would that I lay ;
To be done with the hunger, the toil, and the striving,
    The comfortless night and the desolate day.
Oh, mother in heaven, look down from the glory,
    And take me at last as of old to your breast,
Let me sob in your ears all my pitiful story,
    And then with the angels, and you, be at rest."

A woman sobbed in the very midst of the verse.   The audience sat as if spell-bound until the end, and then electrified the child by such bursts of applause as she had never before received.

Vera hardly deserved their plaudits. She had but seized upon the words and made them her own—she had been indeed the forlorn, neglected child whose mother was in heaven !—

but her hearers believed the impersonation to be simply dramatic, and gave her credit for talent and training which she did not possess.

She could not see Mr. Ravenscroft's face.

He came behind the scenes in a short time, and found Vera in Mrs. Kemp's lap, crying her heart out upon her comfortable bosom.

"What have they done to her? What is the matter?" he thundered.

"I don't know, sir, I'm sure; unless it is the way that that brazen-faced girl struck her just before she sang her first song—I gave her a piece of my mind, the saucy jade!—"

"*Struck* her?" said Gaston. It was well for Julia that she was out of his reach at that moment. His voice, though low, was menacing and stern. "Where is that man?" he said. "He has broken his bargain."

"No, no!" cried Vera, starting up. "It did not hurt me—I was not crying for that!—please don't——"

"What are you crying for, then?" he said gently. "Don't be afraid to tell me, Vera; if that girl has hurt you, she ought to be punished. No? Well, what is the matter?"

" It was only the song, she murmured shame-facedly. "It was so like me—I was really the little girl without any mother—and without any friends, until—until you found me."

And Vera suddenly caught his hand between her own and kissed it, greatly to Mrs. Kemp's astonishment.

He looked at the child gravely, with a faint lifting of his eyebrows; then drew her closer to him with a gentle, caressing gesture.

" Poor child! That life is over for you now, Vera. Forget it as soon as you can. And now come home with me. You have no farewells to make, I suppose?"

" If you would not mind," she faltered, " I should like so much to say good-bye to Davy?"

" Who is Davy?"

" He plays the violin; he is in the band. He is lame, and I love him because he was always so kind to me."

" You shall see him to-morrow at the inn. Have you anything here belonging to you? Get your things together and come."

Vera obeyed him hastily. She saw nothing more of Julia. They met Emily Stanger in one of the corridors: she tossed her head and drew away her skirts as they approached her. Mr. Stanger, in eager conversation with another man stood near the door.

Gaston caught a sentence or two as he passed by.

"Such talent too! Never saw so much in a child of that age—but couldn't afford to refuse, you know——Ah!——"

He started at seeing Mr. Ravenscroft, and bowed with an uneasy crafty smile. Mr. Ravenscroft's hand closed on Vera's a little more tightly than before, but he gave the stage-manager neither look nor word. Mrs. Kemp and Franklyn followed bearing Vera's very few and poor belongings. And so she passed from the tyranny of Jonas Stanger to the guardianship of Gaston Ravenscroft.

When he reached the "Falcon," Mr. Ravenscroft gave some orders which seemed to differ from those previously bestowed. He had arranged at first that Vera should sup with Mrs. Kemp; he now directed that she should take her evening meal with him.

He touched no food himself; but he plied her

with good things until she could eat no more. Then, while the servants took away the dishes, he leaned back in a low armchair, and sank into a melancholy reverie. Vera sat on a high seat at some distance, and watched him furtively; she liked to dwell upon each distinctive trait—the short-cropped hair and close moustache of raven blackness, the bent brows, the strong handsome features, the fine dark eyes. Vera thought her hero a middle-aged man, old enough to be her father. She was quite surprised to learn in after days that he had then been only five and twenty.

He lifted his eyes at last and caught her glance. Immediately he roused himself and stretched out his hand to her.

"Come and sit by me, Vera," he said. She dragged a footstool to his chair and sat down beside him. He stroked her hair as he had done that morning upon the downs. "Child," he said, "I wonder what I am to do with you."

Vera's face fell. She had thought that he had some plan ready. He noticed her change of expression.

"What a sensitive plant it is! Don't be frightened, child. Matters will be arranged for you; never fear.   But you disconcerted all my plans this evening."

"How?" asked Vera.

He laughed.   "I will tell you—in ten years' time, if I know you then, Vera.   Who taught you to sing?"

"Davy," she answered promptly.

"Davy is a wonderful man," he said, with an enigmatic expression on his face.   "Are you fond of singing?"

"Oh, yes.   But there is one thing I should like better."

"What?"

"I want to play the violin.   My father played it.   I have his violin.   And my mother played it too."

"Ah, that accounts for the violin case that puzzled me.   You should have made Davy teach you to play."

"He did—a little."

"Indeed?   Let me hear you play, Vera."

Vera went for her violin, which she handled with care and reverence.   She was nervous about her playing, if not about her singing, because she was not so sure of the effect that she would produce; but she did her best. She played some simple airs that Davy had taught her, then a German volkslied of which her mother had been fond. When she had finished she noted the same inscrutable look of surprise upon Mr. Ravenscroft's face that she had seen before. But he said nothing.

"Don't you like it?" she said at last, very wistfully. "I know I play badly."

He smiled a little, then spoke with the air of one who wishes to counsel wisely.

"You have, no doubt, a talent for music, Vera," he said. "You must cultivate it, of course. But do not let your mind run upon a public life. Your nature is not fitted for it. You would suffer a martyrdom on the stage, poor child! Love music for its own sake, not for the sake of fame or money."

Vera could not understand him, and said so frankly.

"You will understand me in time," he said. "Put away your violin, child, and talk to me. Is it possible that I met you for the first time this morning only? It seems years ago."

"I shall never forget it," she answered. "Nobody has been so good to me before—so kind, so good !”

“That has not been my character heretofore,” he said dryly. And then he fell into a long silence which Vera did not try to break.

“I shall take you home with me to-morrow, Vera,” he said after a time. “You will meet my mother and my sister-in-law. I suppose you understand”—and there was an ironical ring in his voice which Vera did not like—“that you must not treat them with as much frankness as you bestowed upon Miss Stanger.”

“They will not speak to me as Miss Stanger did.”

“I won’t answer for the way in which my mother speaks to you,” said Gaston in an enigmatic tone. “In any case, remember that she is much older than you, and behave to her with respect.” Vera thought the warning unnecessary, and held her peace. “Now go to bed, my child. I left word at the theatre that your friend Davy was to call here in the morning. What is his name beside Davy, by the by ?”

“Davy Rowe.”

“Davy—David Rowe !” said Gaston, with a

sudden change of tone. Vera turned to look at him, but he averted his face, and sat with his cheek upon his hand. "What brings him here?" he murmured to himself dreamily.

Vera waited for a few minutes, but finding that he took no notice of her, she stole quietly away and went to bed.

Gaston sat long in deep abstraction. At last he roused himself, and began to write a letter to Richard Hervey. It was midnight before he had completed the task that he had set himself, but when it was done he felt more satisfaction than had visited his breast for many a day.

"I was a coward to think of ending my troubles in that way," he murmured to himself. "The child saved me. I will do what I can for her."

It was on the next day that Vera received her farewell visit from her friend the fiddler, David Rowe, whom Gaston had known under such different auspices. He came about ten o'clock in the morning. Mr. Ravenscroft had already gone out, leaving word that the musician was to be admitted; and Vera met him in a little back parlour of the Falcon Inn and rapturously threw her arms round his neck.   David Rowe had never suspected that the lady who played a humble part in Mr. Stanger's company was the widowed daughter of Mr. Hervey of Netherby Manor, but he had been attracted to her through her little daughter Vera, whose caresses had won his heart when she was hardly old enough to walk alone. Vera's mother had very possibly recognised David Rowe from the very first : he was less changed than she had been by years of sorrow, poverty, and exile; but if she recognised him she never told him of the fact.   She was always particularly gentle and considerate in her dealings with him ; and she allowed Vera to have more intercourse with the lame fiddler than with any other member of the troupe.   It was Davy, therefore, who had developed Vera's musical talent, and nourished her imagination on a never-failing store of wild legends and ghost stories.   It seemed to him sometimes as if in Vera he had found his Lucy once again, as she had been in the days of her childhood in the cottage at Netherby.   As for Vera, she was sincerely, if somewhat patronisingly, attached to him ; and welcomed his visit with delight, which afforded Davy much satisfaction.

"Stanger's mad with us all this morning, missy," he said confidentially. He says it'll ruin him for you to leave the company."

"He won't turn you off for coming to see me, will he, Davy?"

"It's not much odds if he does. I can get a living anywheres."

"I shall never forget you, Davy, you know."

"Out of sight, out of mind, missy."

"Not with me, Davy dear. You have been so kind to me. Mamma used to say you were a kind man. If ever I am rich, I shall find you out and give you as much money as ever you want."

Davy shook his head but said nothing.

"Don't you think I shall ever be rich?" Vera asked. "I shall work hard and try: I want some money for you and other people."

"Try if you like, but try the right way, dearie. It's ill gained what the devil gives."

"But you don't think that the gentleman means to do me any harm, do you, Davy?" said Vera, gathering from this remark, after some reflection, that Davy thought her in danger.

She had not yet accustomed herself to speaking of Mr. Ravenscroft by his name.

"I can't tell," said Davy meditatively. "It is a queer start altogether. Why should he take you away from Stanger's when he knows nothing whatever about you. It's as queer as Dick's hatband, which went nine times round and wouldn't tie at the last."

"Oh, I've heard of Dick before," cried Vera, almost pettishly. "Who *was* Dick? Why did he want a hat-band? I wish you wouldn't talk of him if you can't say anything more sensible than that."

"Ay, ay; it's always the way. New friends, new manners. It's time I was off."

"No, Davy, no," entreated Vera, clinging to him. "I did not mean to be cross. Be kind to me, Davy; I shall not see you again for a long time perhaps."

"That's true," he said; "truer than you think for, missy. It's all come to an end now. You've been a slave to one man, and now you'll be a slave to another, and the Lord knows whether you'll ever be free to do as you please for the rest of your life."

"What do you mean, Davy ?   I'm not a slave at all."

"You've been bought and sold like one, at any rate," said Davy with bitterness.   "Would Stanger part with you for nothing ? No, it's money that has done it : two hundred pounds or more at the least, as I've heard tell to make you this strange gentleman's apprentice instead of Jonas Stanger's.   He's bought you, and he's your master, and that's the long and the short of it."

"I am glad of it then," said the child passionately.   "I like to do what he tells me. I always shall.   He is good to me, and I love him."

"Love or not, he's your master," returned Davy in an obstinate tone.   "I shall scarce hear much more of you, missy.   I haven't set eyes on this gentleman yet, nor heard his name.   I dare say he's a fine gentleman, by all reports ?"   This was said questioningly.

"Yes, he is a very fine gentleman indeed !" Vera asseverated.   "He is very rich—very handsome—very good ; and his name is Mr. Gaston Ravenscroft."

Davy started from his seat with dilated eyes and outstretched hands.

"What's that you say?" he stammered. "What — what's his name? Ravenscroft — Gaston Ravenscroft of Netherby? The Lord have mercy upon you, child! Is it into the hands of that wicked man that you have fallen?"

"He is not a wicked man, Davy! How can you say so?"

"Because I know—because I know," said the musician with an appearance of great agitation. "I can't tell you why—it's a story that you would not understand; but I know that he's not a man to be trusted. Oh, my dear, what would your mother say to me, as asked me to look after you when she was on her dying bed?"

"I don't believe that Mr. Ravenscroft is anything but good and kind," said Vera, whose eyes were filling with indignant tears. "You are very naughty and disagreeable to tell me so, Davy, and I think it's very wrong of you. Where are you going?"

"My dearie," said the fiddler, shaking his head mournfully, "I can't do anything for you but warn you. *That* I will do, and then I'll go.

Remember that Mr. Ravenscroft is not to be trusted : remember that I say so. He's a bad man and will bring you harm, and do you a mischief if he can. So take care ! "

And with these ominous words David Rowe took leave of Vera.

CHAPTER VIII.

A REBEL.

RAVENSCROFT returned to Netherby without meeting David Rowe, whose presence at Elmstone made the young man doubly anxious to leave that place. He took Vera with him. His plans were not matured with respect to her—in fact, he had scarcely formed any definite ones, for he fully expected that this task would at once be taken off his hands by Mr. Hervey, Madame Waldstein, and Felicia. It did not cross his mind at all that any one of the three might raise an objection to her presence at Netherby.

Vera herself—shy, excited, and almost overwhelmed with the sense of liberty and idleness—did not venture to ask any questions respecting her future. She had already made an idol of her new friend, and thought that all that he

said and did was right. Gaston bestowed little
apparent notice upon her, but he was carelessly
kind and indulgent; and it was plain that the
new interest which she had brought into his life
was of service to him. He was less dispirited
and languid than he had been since the beginning of his illness.

"Stay here, Vera," he said to her, when they
had reached Ravenscroft Hall. He opened the
door of a small sitting-room and pointed to a
chair. "I will come back presently or send for
you. They do not know yet of your arrival; I
must go and prepare their minds."

He left her with a reassuring nod and smile.
Some time elapsed before she heard more of him,
but she did not wait long alone. A little girl,
with a doll in her arms almost as big as herself,
pushed open the door and announced her name
to be "Olivia." With Olivia Ravenscroft—her
second cousin, although she did not know it—
Vera speedily made friends.

Little Olivia was four years old and Vera was
not far wrong when she mentally decided that she
had never seen a lovelier child. The complexion
of peach-like bloom, the tendrils of silky dark

hair clustering round the white forehead and laughing eyes, the delicate features and rosy mouth—nay, even the dainty white frock with its black bows and the look of exquisite care visible in every detail of her attire—all these things impressed Vera with their perfect completeness and a sense of her own poverty and insignificance. She was far more shy than Olivia, but in a few minutes the two children became quite at ease with each other, and chatted and played together as if they had been intimate all their lives.

Their games were, however, presently interrupted. For some time the sound of voices had issued stormily from the next room. Then came the rattle of rings as a curtain was drawn aside, and then a door was hastily flung open. Little Olivia rose from the floor, with a solemn look in her great dark eyes, as she said to Vera wisely:

"That is grandmamma."

Folding-doors stretched across on one side of the room, and these were the doors that opened to admit Madame Waldstein and her son. The Baroness entered leaning on Gaston's arm; Felicia came behind them with a white shawl thrown over her arm. Madame Waldstein was queen of the household, and it was plain that every member of it must be prepared to pay her assiduous attention. She was a very handsome old lady, and she did not at all disdain the use of art to heighten her charms, although these were wonderfully little impaired by time. Her face was like a piece of delicate old china, her white hair was dressed in a multitude of little curls high above her forehead, her dark eyes flashed vivaciously beneath eyebrows which nature would scarcely have left so dark and well defined. It was very easy to see from whom Olivia Ravenscroft inherited her most characteristic traits.

She was dressed in mourning for her elder son; but she had resumed her usual ornaments— diamonds—of which she was extravagantly fond. The lace on her head was kept in its place upon the frizzled curls by magnificent diamond pins; there were diamonds in her ears, at her throat, and upon her wrinkled white fingers. When she came suddenly into the sunshiny room in which the children were playing, it seemed to Vera as if some wonderful fairy god-mother of legendary lore stood before her all radiant with points of changing light: ready to change persons who displeased her into singing birds and coloured fish, or to transport herself, at a moment's notice, a thousand miles away. When she came to know Madame Waldstein a little better, she was glad to reflect that she had at least no supernatural powers; for this old lady seldom used her abilities for any very benevolent purpose. Felicia, walking behind her mother-in-law, was tall and slender, with an oval face of Madonna-like sweetness, and tender melancholy eyes; but she was eclipsed by the Baroness, although she had youth upon her side.

"Is this the child then?" said Madame Waldstein, continuing her conversation with Gaston as she advanced into the room. "What an odd little creature!—Hervey won't have anything to do with her, Gaston; you need not imagine it."

"I expect that he will."

"Not he. He was too angry at the whole business to relent now. I daresay he will furnish money enough for——"

"Pray remember what I told you," Gaston

interrupted with small ceremony. " I have said nothing to her as yet—she does not know——"

He caught Vera's eyes and stopped short in some confusion. She was listening intently and trying to comprehend.

" Let her go into the garden," said the Baroness sharply. " She has eyes like the wolf in the story-book. What an absurdity the whole matter is ! What a game at cross-purposes !" and she laughed satirically.

" I don't understand you," remarked Gaston.

" No ; I daresay not," said his mother, allowing him to lead her to a large arm-chair. " You seldom do, my dear Gaston, and in this case—— Do send the children away, Felicia ; we do not want them here."

The little girls were accordingly banished, and their elders discussed the child's circumstances and prospects with freedom. Gaston was somewhat surprised to find that Felicia did not hail the notion of Vera's remaining at the Hall as a companion for Olivia with any great delight. It was tacitly agreed, however, that she should stay for a time, so that Mrs. Ravenscroft might see what kind of child she was ; but that Vera

should not be told of her relationship to Mr.
Hervey until Mr. Hervey himself had answered
Gaston's letter.

Meantime the children had tea in a dainty
nursery under the supervision of a cheerful-looking nurse, who brushed Vera's hair and tied a
pinafore round her neck exactly as she did to
her own little charge. Mrs. Ravenscroft came
in once to caress her little girl and speak softly
to the visitor. The house was quiet, yet full of
pleasantness. Vera did not respond to the
advances made to her; she was in a shy mood,
almost a fierce one; she wished herself back upon
the stage, where she could be, like little Olivia,
a fairy princess. Then she was angry that Mr.
Ravenscroft had not been near her all the afternoon. Was he forgetting her altogether? Vera
was no heroine; only an untrained, wayward
child; and she was hurt and angry by his treatment of her. It was in no gracious mood that
she went downstairs with pretty little Olivia to
dessert. The nurse had decked her out with a
muslin pinafore and a sash; but she would rather
have worn her old brown frock without disguise.

The Baroness sat in a throne-like chair at one side of the round table ; her son fronted her, and Mrs. Ravenscroft was between them. The air was cool and the light fading ; sweet scents and sounds came through the open window. The table itself was a pretty sight, with its ornaments of flowers, silver, china and crystal, the piles of crimson and purple fruit, the translucent wines reflecting sunset tints upon the snowy table-cloth. Mr. Ravenscroft called Vera to sit by him, and gave her some strawberries. He did not look either pleased or happy, and for some time sat perfectly silent.

Olivia had seated herself by her mother, and chattered gleefully without seeming to expect an answer. It startled every one when the Baroness suddenly tapped the table with her fan and up-lifted her cracked vivacious treble.

"You say that child can sing, Gaston. Let her sing to me ; I used to be a judge of voices. Let me hear her."

"You can scarcely judge of the voice of a child who is not ten years old," said her son dryly.

" I can make allowances," said Madame Waldstein, nodding at him. "And I can judge whether she has talent or not. Now, child, sing."

Vera bent her head over her plate and fingered her strawberries.

"Does she not hear?" said the Baroness, sharply. "Or is she obstinate?"

"She is shy," said Mr. Ravenscroft, without looking at the child. "Sing something, Vera. Anything you know."

The tone was quietly imperious. Suddenly Davy's ill-judged words had recurred to Vera's mind. Mr. Ravenscroft was her master, but she would not be his slave. She would not sing.

"Don't press her, Gaston," said Mrs. Ravens- croft softly. "She does not like it."

"Nonsense!" said Madame Waldstein, in a tone of malicious enjoyment. "I want to hear her, Gaston. Have you no authority over the child whom you say you have 'rescued'? Are my wishes to be set at naught by that baby?"

Mr. Ravenscroft's face grew dark. Even Vera could see that his mother had offended him. He did not look round at her, however; he only said, more curtly than ever:

"Sing, Vera."

She did not dare to disobey. But it was left to her to choose what she should sing; and, out of pure freakishness, she selected the song that she knew Mr. Ravenscroft had not liked when he heard it at the theatre. There was no harm in it, but there was a good deal of slang; more, indeed, than she herself could understand. She sang it with the verve and spirit which Mr. Stanger's company had found acceptable. The Baroness laughed to herself; Mrs. Ravenscroft looked at the little girl with a sort of incredulity mingled with positive alarm; her brother-in-law's brow gathered blackness. At the end of one verse he bade Vera stop. "That is enough," he said.

"Quite enough, I think," said Mrs. Ravenscroft, putting her arm round the wondering Olivia, and pushing back her chair from the table. "Is that the kind of song you like to hear, Gaston?"

"There's no harm in the song, my dear," said Madame Waldstein briskly. "A trifle slangy and vulgar; that is all. A low music-hall ditty, I should think. Go on, child. I like my dishes highly spiced. I can put up with a touch of coarseness in the seasoning. I love onions and peppermint."

"My tastes differ from yours, mother," said Mrs. Ravenscroft, with dignity. "If you will excuse me I will take Olivia up to the nursery. It is time for her to go to bed."

"And for Vera too," said Mr. Ravenscroft indifferently.

Mrs. Ravenscroft stopped, looked at the Baroness for a moment with an odd expression of appeal, then left the room holding her little girl by the hand. At a sign from Mr. Ravenscroft, Vera followed her. She felt that in some way she had made a mistake, and was miserable at the thought; and yet she scarcely understood what was wrong.

She went with lagging steps into the day-nursery, whither Olivia and her mother had preceded her. Mrs. Ravenscroft at once entered the adjoining bedroom, and shut the door of communication between the two rooms. The nurse was absent; for some little time Vera remained alone. Mrs. Ravenscroft went down-stairs again, and the child looked out of the window, cooled her flushed cheeks in the evening breeze, and wondered where she was to sleep and what Mr. Ravenscroft would ultimately do with her.

It was all but dark when Mrs. Ravenscroft reappeared. She was moving more quickly than usual ; and her voice had an agitated sound which she vainly tried to disguise by a forced cheerfulness.

"Your hat and cloak are here, are they not ? Mr. Ravenscroft will be ready in five minutes, and you are to go with him."

"To go away ?" said Vera, moving from the window and coming close to her. "Must I go ? I thought I might stay here, perhaps—just for a little time—with your little girl."

Felicia's face was flushed. She answered with a touch of stiffness, "My little girl has her own companions. You are going to school very shortly." And then something overcame the attempt to be cold and hard. "Oh, you poor little thing!" she said, sitting down and drawing the child to her lap. "It is not your fault. You have no mother." And then she kissed her, and Vera felt the tears wet upon her cheeks.

This was all utterly incomprehensible to Vera,

but she leaned her face against Mrs. Ravenscroft's
shoulder, and felt comforted by the pressure of
her soft maternal arms. " I should like to stay
with you," she said, almost in a whisper. Felicia
gave the child another caress, but answered nothing.

While Vera was putting on her hat and
cloak, however, Mrs. Ravenscroft talked to her
gently—told her to be a good girl and learn her
lessons, and not sing silly songs—such as she
had heard in the theatre—for they would get her
into trouble with older and wiser people. Mr.
Ravenscroft took a great interest in her (she said
nothing about the relationship), and would probably send her to school and afterwards find her
a situation as a governess, perhaps, if she behaved nicely and learned the things that it was
good for girls to know ; and she would always
help Vera, if it was in her power to do so.   Then,
seeing possibly how forlorn and bewildered poor
little Vera felt, she kissed her again, and put into
her hands a string of coral beads which she had
admired on Olivia's neck that afternoon, and told
her to keep them in remembrance of the little
girl.

As Vera left the nursery, Felicia stole softly into the other room, and bent over a little white bed in which her own child was lying. Vera could not see this without remembering the visits that her mother used to pay her in the darkness when she was in bed. She turned away with a sudden constriction of her throat, a clenching of her hands, a resolute forcing back of the tears in her hot eyes. For although she was dismissed with tears and kisses and a gift, she felt instinctively that she was dismissed in disgrace; she was no fit companion for Olivia Ravenscroft.

A servant conducted her to the front door. Here stood Mr. Ravenscroft, eyeing a powerful black horse that had just been brought to the steps. Vera took her place timidly beside him. At first he did not see her; then he started and said, "Oh, here you are, child!" and mounted his horse. "Help her up, Norris," he said to the man. And before she well knew what she was doing, she had been half-lifted, half-swung up, and found herself before him upon the horse's back.

He put his arm round her, and she felt herself safe enough; but there was something in the novelty of the situation that kept her quiet. They had gone for some distance before he spoke.

"Are you comfortable?" he said at last.

"Yes, sir, thank you."

Vera's tone was a very humble one. He glanced down at her and saw the tears on her eyelashes.

"What did Mrs. Ravenscroft say to you?" he asked abruptly.

"She told me to be a good girl and—and—not to sing," Vera answered tremulously. "She was very kind."

"Oh, was she?" Then, breaking out into a short laugh: "What possessed you, Vera, to go and sing a song of that sort? Of course it prejudiced them against you. The odd thing is that I have watched you for two or three days, and could have sworn that you were as well-behaved and gentle and refined as Felicia's own child herself! And you broke out to-night like——" he did not finish the sentence.

Vera could not speak, so he continued grimly: "Well, we have ruined your chances in that house at least. I thought I could have induced them to take you in, adopt you, pet you, make you Olivia's playmate. But you set Olivia's mother against you, my dear, and I offended the Baroness; and between us we made a mess of the whole affair. So nothing remains but that I should take you over to the inn at Mickleham, and keep you there for a day or two till I find another home for you; and if you are asked to sing henceforward, I should advise you to choose the pathetic, not the comic, line of performances. Women in the country have no sense of humour."

He might have proceeded in this vein for some time but for an involuntary little sob that escaped the child. He stopped abruptly.

"There!" he said after a pause, during which she had much ado to repress the sobs which were shaking her from head to foot, "there, child, don't cry! What they say or think signifies nothing either to you or to me. What a queer little mortal you are! All fire and fury one moment, and then dissolved in tears! Do you think I have never quarrelled with those good people before? Come, dry your tears, and tell me why you would not sing at first when I asked you to-night?"

Vera got out an answer with difficulty. "Old Davy said I was your—your slave; and you were my master. I remembered it when you told me to sing; and it made me angry."

He maintained silence for some moments, but when she glanced timidly up at his face, he was smiling.

"Davy is a fool," he said finally. "I have no ambition to be a slave-owner, Vera. I don't mean to pose as your master, tutor, father, or anything else authoritative. But you are rather young to begin this work of rebellion at such a rapid rate. First, Stanger; now, myself——"

"Oh!" cried little Vera, "I would do any-thing for you; indeed, I would!"

"Except sing? Now there's nothing to cry about; indeed, if you cry any more I shall put you down in the road and leave you to your own devices—probably find you next morning drowned in a pool of your own tears. There, forget your grief for a time, if you can, poor little bird. I will take care of you."

He spoke with tenderness which he had never shown to her before, and Vera nestled more closely to him as they rode onwards in the moonlight. He did not speak again. He was much vexed by the turn which things had taken. Felicia had refused to have the little waif and stray in the house with her child for more than a night or two, and the Baroness had upheld her in that decision. The upshot had been a tremendous quarrel, followed by Gaston's resolution to carry Vera away at once and take charge of her until Mr. Hervey's letter should be received. Accordingly, he took her to the chief hotel in Mickleham and remained there for the next two or three days. She gave him little trouble. The events of the preceding days had produced a curious effect upon her: she became positively ill, and lay in bed for some days in a motionless, half-unconscious state—the result of over exertion and excitement—during which he could do nothing but relinquish her to the care of a nurse. Before she was well the expected letter came to Gaston from Mr. Hervey. It was not a satisfactory one. Mr. Hervey wished to know nothing and see nothing of his granddaughter; but he was willing to pay her expenses at a good school if one could be found for her. He was prepared to be liberal, but he was not affectionate.

In a wonderfully short time the school was found. Thither Vera was despatched with a handsome outfit, of which Felicia (a little remorseful for her behaviour to the orphaned child) took charge. Nothing was said to Vera about her family or her mother's history : it was thought wise to reserve this communication until she should be older and better able to understand it. In the meantime she was allowed to think of Mr. Ravenscroft as her guardian and generous benefactor.

Gaston thought little about her. He had made up his mind to leave England for a time ; and before she had been a week at school he started for the East. Many years elapsed before he set foot on English soil again.

CHAPTER IX.

NEW FRIENDS AND OLD.

Gaston Ravenscroft had vanished from the scene, and was little missed, except by the child whom he had rescued from an unhappy and unsatisfactory life. She indeed mourned for his absence, and made a hero of him in her thoughts; but by no one else was he much regretted. Little was heard of him for the next few years.

Meanwhile Vera Marlitt remained at the school where he had placed her. She soon forgot her experiences of the stage or became ashamed of them, but her love for music grew with her growth until it became a passion. Seeing this, her schoolmistress (who from time to time corresponded with Mrs. Philip Ravenscroft with respect to Vera) recommended that she should have special instruction in that subject. It seemed that no expense was to be spared in Vera's education. She was to learn everything, and to have her powers cultivated to the utmost. At fifteen she went to a great German Conservatoire; thence to Italy, chiefly for the purpose of cultivating her voice, which was a remarkably good one. After a time she returned to England, and established herself in London with her old schoolmistress, Mrs. Cradock, who had given up teaching. The introductions and testimonials that she brought with her to England soon made her known in musical circles. She sang at concerts, in drawing-rooms, she gave lessons, she worked steadily and hard; and in time she found that she was achieving a tolerable measure of success. And then she carried out a purpose which had long been uppermost in her mind—the purpose of severing herself from all dependence upon Gaston Ravenscroft.

This action of hers was less ungracious than it may seem. Gaston, feeling annoyed at his inability to tell her the whole story of her grandfather's cold liberality as regarded money matters, had repulsed with some harshness her attempts to express her gratitude to *him*. She had written once, pouring out the affection and thankfulness which she felt, from a full heart; and the only reply which she had received had been a curt message through her schoolmistress to the effect that he needed no thanks, and did not wish her to write to him again upon the subject. Vera wrote once more—when she had fixed upon her profession; but to this letter she obtained no sort of reply. And again, when she felt that she had secured her own position and might well consider herself independent of his help, she wrote a few lines to inform him of her success, and to ask him to discontinue his remittances to her. She knew that she was guilty of a somewhat rash act in trying to loose herself from the hand which had certainly been stretched out to help her for many years; but Vera was proud, and despised gifts that were thrown to her without affection, as one might throw a bone to a hungry dog. Therefore she wrote to Mr. Ravenscroft on this wise :—

"You have forbidden me to thank you for all that you have done," she said, "but you must at least allow me to explain why I have returned to your bankers the sum so generously placed at my disposal at the beginning of the year. I need accept your gifts no longer. I have the means of earning my own living, and need be a burden upon no one. I have more engagements than I have time to fulfil, and am not likely to be in want of help at present. I must for the last time ask you to let me thank you from the bottom of my heart for all that you have done for me, and to believe that I remain always, gratefully and sincerely yours—VERA MARLITT."

When she had sent this letter to Beyrout, from which place all letters to Gaston were to be forwarded, she felt more contented than she had done for many a long day. She was young and strong and able to work for herself: the sense of independence was very precious to her. She had Mrs. Cradock for a companion in pleasant lodgings in Kensington, and she was gradually making friends for herself in many circles beside purely musical ones. She had a great number of acquaintances by whom she was liked and esteemed, and there was little doubt but that her reputation as a concert singer would become greater year by year as time went on. At two and twenty she had been fortunate indeed to achieve as much success as had already fallen to her lot.

It was a fine afternoon in April, and she was coming away from a rehearsal, in company with Mrs. Cradock, when an unexpected hindrance occurred. Mrs. Cradock suddenly laid her hand on Vera's arm, and spoke rather nervously:

"Do you know the young man who is looking at you so intently, Vera?"

"Not at all."

"How pertinaciously he stares! He is quite rude. Get into the cab, Vera, dear. Oh, he is coming this way. What can he want? is he begging?"

Mrs. Cradock had already taken her seat in the cab, and Vera was about to follow her, when the young man of whom they had spoken drew near, hat in hand, with an evident desire to speak.

Vera glanced at him in surprise. He addressed her by the name which she still used in public, the name by which she had been known in Mr. Stanger's company. "I think," he said, "that I have the honour of speaking to Mademoiselle de Lusignan?"

Vera bowed assent.

"May I convey to mademoiselle a message

from an old friend of hers who is also a friend of mine ?"

"An old friend of mine !" Of whom did the stranger speak? Vera wondered whether she had met this young man or his friends abroad : certainly she did not remember his face. She was sure that he was not an Englishman, although he seemed to speak English perfectly ; but there was some trick of manner or gesture that stamped him in her mind as a foreigner. His voice was strikingly musical; his demeanour quiet, polished, refined. But although he had the characteristics of a gentleman in voice and bearing, it was noticeable that his clothes were exceedingly old and shabby. He was poor, he was not an Englishman—two facts that were decidedly against him in Mrs. Cradock's opinion, and as strongly in his favour in that of Vera.

Whilst Vera still hesitated for a reply, Mrs. Cradock spoke, and, misunderstanding the situation completely, she spoke sharply :

"Go away, my good man ; the lady has nothing for you. Take your hand off the door. Drive on, cabman."

" Wait, cabman—hush, dear—it is not what

you think," Vera said, feeling her face grow hot at this mistake. "I beg your pardon; you said that you had a message for me?"

"Yes," he said, "from David Rowe."

"David Rowe?"

"You knew him, he tells me, by the name of old Davy the fiddler."

"Dear old Davy! yes, yes!" cried Vera. "Where is he? I have wanted so much to find him again! Is he in London?"

"He is in London, but he is very ill. He saw your name advertised, I believe"—the stranger spoke very deferentially—"and felt sure that you must be the Mademoiselle Vera de Lusignan whom he knew as a child. He sends you this little token;" and Vera saw the half of a coin which she and Davy had broken before they parted, "and begs me to ask you whether you would have the infinite kindness to honour him with a visit, as he cannot come to you."

"Certainly: of course I will. I will go at once. Where does he live?"

The stranger named a street which Vera did not know, but at which Mrs. Cradock looked horrified.

"My dear Vera, in the lowest neighbourhood! You cannot possibly go!"

"I assure you," said the young man eagerly, "that there is no danger. The street is perfectly safe and quiet, although poor. I shall be happy to accompany you. I—I—" he hesitated for a moment, and then added firmly, "I live there myself."

Mrs. Cradock surveyed him keenly. She was astonished. The stranger returned her gaze very frankly, but with a faint smile not devoid of irony.

Vera also examined his face more closely than she had done before. He was still uncovered, and the sunshine fell upon a very handsome fair head and an attractive countenance, full of the glow of manliness, full also of a curious calm and sweetness which inspired confidence. The features were fine but a little worn; his mouth was perhaps the finest and the sweetest feature of all, although the drooping fair moustache left its expression sometimes enigmatical. His eyes were gray or blue—one could not be certain which; pleasant, thoughtful eyes, now lighted by quiet humour, which was as free from bitterness as from guile. There was indeed something so genial and so trustworthy about this man's face that Vera liked him on the spot. And in her heart of hearts so did Mrs. Cradock, although she thought it her duty to raise objections.

"I will go," Vera said quickly. "You will come with me, Aunt Dorothy, will you not? And you, sir, may we give you a seat? You can then kindly direct the cabman where to go, if he should be in any difficulty."

He thanked her, but seemed inclined to take his seat on the box beside the driver, saying that by so doing he could insure their reaching their destination by the shortest route. This the two ladies would not allow. Before he entered the cab, however, he presented Mrs. Cradock with a card on which his name was written in pencil: "Maurice Guyon."

As they drove rapidly eastward, Vera asked him several questions about her old friend. He said that Davy had been ill for some time, and that his present ailment was a sort of low fever. This, however, was in itself slight, and the real danger lay in the breaking up of his constitution, long undermined by hard work and exposure.

Davy's lodging was in a squalid-looking house in a street near the Strand. The visitors entered a bare, scantily-furnished room at the top of the house; poor enough, but scrupulously neat and clean. Upon an uncomfortable - looking pallet lay Davy, his emaciated face turned eagerly towards the opening door, his wasted fingers clutching the neck of the cherished violin that still lay at his side. He held out his hands to Vera as she came in. She rushed forward to kneel at his bedside and kiss his grizzled face as she had done when last she saw him at Elmstone.

"Dear Davy," she said, "you remember Vera, do you not? I would have come before if I had known where you were. Oh, why did you not let me hear? Don't you remember what we used to say? how we used to plan that when I was a singer I would find you out and take you home, and make you happy and comfortable all the days of your life? The time has come, Davy. I am able to do it now. You will come home with me, will you not?"

He was holding her hands in his, and smiling from time to time with a wonderfully radiant face. He nodded once or twice, and moved her hands gently up and down, then turned his beaming eyes upon Mr. Guyon who stood with Mrs. Cradock at the foot of the bed.

"I told you so," he said triumphantly; "I told you she'd come! She wouldn't forget her old Davy—not if she lived a thousand years! You were wrong and I was right. My sweet little lady, so you've come at last, and found your voice and your fortune as I said you would!"

"Yes, Davy," Vera said. "But who told you that I would not come? Did you not know that I would have done anything to find you? I tried, dear Davy, but I did not succeed. You never thought that I had forgotten you?"

"No, my pretty, no. He didn't know you as I did. It was *he* that thought you would not come." He nodded towards Maurice Guyon, who was watching the scene silently and attentively, and at whom Vera flashed a glance of impulsive indignation.

But as she could not call a stranger to

account for his words, she laid her lips on Davy's hand in mute protest: he understood her and smiled.

"I can only ask your pardon, mademoiselle," said Mr. Guyon respectfully. "I see indeed that I was much mistaken."

"They said you were proud, dearie," Davy murmured. "Proud and cold. But I knew what they meant. It was always your way to be silent: you were never the one to scream and cry even when Stanger beat you, were you? Cold and proud you might be to those you did not love: never cold and never proud to your old Davy who taught you how to sing!"

"Never, Davy, never."

"My dear," Mrs. Cradock nervously interposed, "do you not think that your presence excites this poor man too much? Perhaps you had better come away now. We will send for a doctor and a nurse if you think well. No doubt he requires proper care and attention."

"Yes, *my* care and attention," Vera said. "We will send for everything he needs, but I am not yet ready to go away, dear auntie, although you can go if you like."

"Who is she?" said Davy strangely. "Your aunt—your own relation?"

"No," Vera answered. "Only by adoption." And she saw his face fall at her response.

Meanwhile Mrs. Cradock, almost in tears, was reduced to appealing to Mr. Guyon. "*I* do not want to go," she said, "but I wish Mademoiselle de Lusignan would come away. Her health is so precious! And she is not strong. If she were to catch an illness I should never forgive myself."

Mr. Guyon smiled reassuringly. "The doctor assures me, Madame, that there is nothing infectious in our friend's disorder. Otherwise, I would not have brought Mademoiselle de Lusignan hither. Allow me to offer you a chair. If mademoiselle will tell me at what hour she would like her carriage summoned I will arrange that it shall be at the door."

He spoke as if Mademoiselle de Lusignan had been a princess and her homely four-wheeler a state chariot. Vera was half amused and half displeased: she suspected him of irony, but saw no trace of it in his frank and kindly eyes. She turned to Mrs. Cradock.

"Let the cab take you home, Aunt Dorothy," she said. "Let me stay here and nurse Davy. I can get a room close by. I will sleep here and take care of him till we find a nurse or take him out to Kensington."

But even Davy opposed this plan.

"No, my dear, it ain't for the likes of you," he said. "A nurse?—why, I've got a real good one. Mr. Maurice, there, sits up with me at nights, gives me my medicine, brings me the news and makes me laugh; and what could a nurse do more? Don't you go to needless expense for an old man like me. Stay here for half an hour or so, and come and see me to-morrow if you like: that's all I want."

"You could not stay here, mademoiselle," Mr. Guyon assured her. "The place is not fit."

"If it is fit for Davy," Vera answered vehemently, "it is fit for me."

"My dear Vera!" Mrs. Cradock expostulated. "I am sure that Mr. Guyon is quite right."

"Shall I say 'in an hour,' mademoiselle?" said Mr. Guyon. And Vera yielded, not being well able to do otherwise.

"I shall be at hand if you should want me,

Madame," he said with a bow. But Davy's thin voice interposed.

"Come back when you have ordered the cab, won't you, sir? I want you here. He has been a true friend to me, dearie, and I like to see him by me. Besides, it's his room, not mine."

Mrs. Cradock added her entreaty. "Oh yes, pray come back. We would not turn you out of your own room on any account; and indeed, I feel safer when you are here."

Mr. Guyon bowed, glanced at Vera, and then replied that he would return in a few minutes.

Vera could not refrain, when he was out of the room, from putting a question which had been troubling her mind for some time.

"Who is this Mr. Guyon, Davy?"

"I don't know, my pretty," said the fiddler, shaking his head. "He's a foreign chap, and he's in trouble, and he's poor. That's all I know. But he won't always be poor: I've read so much in his hand; for I can tell fortunes, you know, missy. Anyhow he's a good man and a gentleman. And now about yourself, dearie. Tell old Davy what's happened to you during the last twelve years."

Vera gave him a short sketch of her history, to which he listened with great satisfaction. Mr. Guyon returned before it was ended, but did not appear to attend to it. He went to the open window and leaned out.

" And so you sing at concerts now, do you, my pretty ?"

" Yes, Davy."

" And they throw you flowers and jewels, do they ?"

" Flowers sometimes."

" And you ride in your own carriage ?"

"Why, no, Davy. I am not rich enough for that."

" But you will be one day. And to think that I taught you once! You'll have forgotten all the songs you learned from me, won't you ?"

" No, Davy, I remember them very well."

" Sing me one before you go, missy !"

" Which one, Davy ?"

" Any : I don't care which."

It was hard to sing at that moment, but Vera would have done anything to please him. She chose the song of the motherless child which Mr. Ravenscroft had heard in the little theatre at Elmstone.

Although she subdued her voice as much as possible, it seemed to fill the little room. For one moment, towards the close, she allowed it to swell out to its full power, then to sink to the lowest whisper with the most finished cadence of which it was capable. Vera had sung to crowded audiences with less care and earnestness than she bestowed upon the song that she sang to Davy.

Her pains were rewarded. Davy lay rapt in mute delight; Mrs. Cradock wiped the tears from her eyes; Maurice Guyon stood erect in an attitude of profound attention. His face was somewhat moved, but Vera was glad to find that he did not thank her when she had finished; she had not sung for him.

"I taught you that, did I?" said Davy, dreamily. "Wonderful! wonderful!—it is like the singing of angels. I should like to hear you at the great concerts too, dearie."

"So you shall, Davy. When you are better you shall have tickets as often as you please. I will sing my best for you."

He shook his head sadly.

"I wish I could, my dear; but it's too late

now. And you sang that song when Mr. Ravenscroft heard you, did you not?"

"Yes."

"Where is Mr. Ravenscroft now?"

"I don't know. Somewhere in the East."

"When did you last see him, missy?"

"Twelve years ago, Davy."

The old man drew a long breath, and turned his hollow eyes full upon the girl. "But he writes to you? He is coming to see you soon, now that you are a woman grown—you are great friends?"

Vera's face grew hot. "No, Davy," she answered gently; "Mr. Ravenscroft and I are not friends. He was generous to me, but not—not—kind. I owe him much; but I hope and pray that we may never meet again."

The passion of wounded feeling that lay within her dormant awoke, and roused itself to fuller life even while she spoke. But Davy's face grew bright.

"All the better," he said. "He wouldn't have done you any good, my pretty. Let him be buried in the desert and drowned in the deep seas a thousand times over before ever he brings any harm to you, my little lady. He is not for you."

"He would not harm me. He meant to be kind," Vera answered sadly.

"Kind! With the kindness of the creeper that sucks out the life from the plant that cherishes it! If that is kindness, then Mr. Ravenscroft is kind."

Vera was silent; and in the silence her eyes began, almost for the first time, to scrutinize the apartment in which she sat. Signs of poverty were apparent; but there was at least one indication of the presence of some one beside the fiddler, and of a man not altogether used to poverty. Upon the wall hung the miniature of a very fair and beautiful woman in a gold frame studded with brilliants. It was battered enough, and many of the stones had dropped out; but the setting had once been of the most exquisite and delicate kind. It was not the sort of thing that had ever belonged to Davy.

When Mr. Guyon had gone to summon Vera's cab, she could not resist asking a question about the miniature.

"It's not mine, dearie; it's Mr. Guyon's."

"But *he* does not live here?" Vera queried in surprise.

"He's done so for the last six weeks, my pretty. He's been a kind friend to old Davy, has Maurice Guyon," the musician answered simply.

CHAPTER X.

AN EXILE.

VERA saw that her poor old friend was sadly exhausting his small stock of strength in this conversation, and she resolved to protract it no longer. She took her leave, promising to come again as soon as possible ; but before she went she consulted Mr. Guyon concerning Davy's illness and requirements. It appeared that Mr. Guyon had hitherto been nursing him ; but he acknowledged, with something like a sigh, that he was not able to do for a sick man all that should be done. He himself was obliged to be out very often, especially in the evenings, and a nurse's services were much required.

"I would gladly sit up with him day and night," said the young man, with what seemed to be real and deep emotion: "but my business calls me away at times, and then I can do nothing. You do not know, mademoiselle, what a friend and consoler I have found in Davy and his violin. If you knew, you would not wonder that I long to do for him all that needs to be done; or how bitterly I regret that it lies no longer in my power to do so."

Vera could not help wondering how poor old Davy had been so great a friend to him; but he said nothing more.

She went away to order fruit and flowers, and anything that she thought could add to Davy's pleasure. She found out the doctor who attended him, and heard his opinion of the case—it was not likely to be a lengthy one, he said; she found, also, at his recommendation, a good trustworthy nurse, and despatched her at once to her old friend's lodging; then she turned homeward, still with a heavy heart; for she loved Davy as she had loved him when she was a child, and he would not be with her long.

When Vera visited Davy's room again she found the nurse installed. The character of the place was changed already: a woman's presence made it less bare and squalid. Mr. Guyon was away, so she sat down beside the old man's bed and talked to him for some little time.

By and by her curiosity found its vent.

"Where did you make Mr. Guyon's acquaintance, Davy dear?"

"At a club, missy?"

"At a club?"

"A working man's club. He goes about a good deal among them sort of places, foreign as well as English. A sort of socialist, you know, in his talk; and he talks very well too. And always a kind word for a man, and would share his last crust cheerful-like with a beggar in the street."

"So you made his acquaintance?——" Vera paused, hardly knowing how to frame the question that she wished to put.

"He made mine, dearie. He took a fancy to my playing, and he used to ask me to play the same tunes to him time after time, and listen to them with the tears in his eyes too. And he can play too—wild tunes that you'd think the devil himself had got into, and then again, notes that make you think of all the sadness in the world, and all the love and joy—ay, he's a fine player——"

" Does he ever play in public ?"

" No, dearie : he laughed and shook his head when I asked him that, and said that he couldn't play well enough, and he preferred to be a poor man and a vagabond. That's just it," said Davy dreamily, " he *prefers* to live like me—it's a re'glar gentleman's whim, isn't it ? They do have odd fancies now and again, these gentle-folks."

Vera was silent for a time. " He said that you had been kind to him : how was that, Davy ?"

" You didn't think old Davy could have been kind to anybody, did you dearie ? "

" Indeed I did, Davy."

" Well, I did what he asked me—that was all." A shadow seemed to fall over the rugged face with its hollow eyes and large weird features as he spoke. " I told him he wasn't fit for the work ; but he said he wanted to try all kinds of work that he might know how the workers felt. A gentleman's fad, my dear, that was all. He has lived here ever since I fell ill. That was a gentleman's fancy too : he used to have better rooms than mine."

"What work does he do?" Vera asked curiously.

"He'll tell you—he'll tell you," Davy answered a little peevishly. "Sing to me before you go : I want to hear you. I can't talk any longer."

She sang for a little time to him; but she was soon obliged to go; as she had already stayed longer than she had meant to do. As soon as she left Davy's house she looked round for a cab. But in this narrow and miserable street no cab was to be seen, and she walked onward, expecting every moment to reach a more frequented thoroughfare.

Vera was not gifted with the faculty of easily finding her way in a new place. Through some inaccuracy of memory she missed the right turning, and soon found herself involved in a network of tiny streets and alleys of the less reputable kind, peopled moreover with men and women of no pleasant appearance. A cab crawling leisurely down a more respectable street in the distance excited her hopes ; but it was out of sight before she could attract the cabman's attention. She was late for rehearsal already : evidently she

should have to miss it altogether unless she could
find her way. Moreover on putting her hand
into her pocket to make sure that her purse
was safe, she found that it had mysteriously
disapppeared.

It was no very formidable position to be in,
for Vera knew that she could not be very far
from a respectable neighbourhood, and that her
purse had contained nothing but a few shillings
and some stamps; but the annoyance of the
moment was great, and was imprinted very
legibly upon her flushed and discomfited countenance, when she beheld before her the welcome
face and figure of a man whose name at least she
knew.   It was Mr. Maurice Guyon, walking
leisurely and easily, as if he were familiar with
the place.   He lifted his hat, giving it a sweep
with his arm which almost made her smile—a
flourish so thoroughly un-English that it carried
her mind back at once to the days of her school-
life in Germany; and then he would have passed
without a word, had Vera not uttered his name
in an accent of appeal.

"Can I do anything for you, mademoiselle?"
he said, turning eagerly.

"I am very sorry to trouble you," she answered, "but I have been foolish enough to lose my way—and my purse as well. Will you kindly tell me which is the direction I ought to take? I am going—at least I wish to go—towards Piccadilly."

"Will you allow me to guide you?" he asked. "We are now not very far from the Strand, but you are wandering in an opposite direction from the way that you ought to take; and—excuse me—I do not think that this neighbourhood is very safe for a lady walking alone."

Vera assured him that she would be glad of his guidance, and they went on their way together. They soon fell into talk about Davy, and Vera said that Davy had told her of his love for the violin.

"Davy has genius," he said. "It is a pity that he has had so few chances in life : he might have made a name."

"You are a musician too, he tells me."

"I ought not to be called so," he said, shaking his head. "I play a little, and I am a great lover of music. Certainly, at present I am—well, I may, by stretch of imagination, call myself a

musician, mademoiselle; and it was in gaining
me the position that I now occupy that Davy did
me such service."

"Davy!" Vera exclaimed in astonishment.

" Davy, and no one else," said her companion
with a slightly amused air.   " In truth, mademoiselle, I was reduced to great straits when Davy
met me at the club.   I had begun to think of
begging of my friends for a livelihood.   But
you know that Davy was connected with a
theatre.   A friend of his took an interest in me
—kind of him, was it not?—and obtained for
me a situation at the same house as a violinist in
the band. Oh yes, I think I may call myself a
musician!   I owe that to Davy, who helped me
out of his own slender store when I had not a
kopeck in my pockets."

Hitherto he had spoken lightly, even playfully ; but at the last words his tone changed to
one of deep and grateful feeling.   "Davy is one
of the truest friends I have," he said heartily.

" But surely"—Vera paused in some little
embarrassment—" surely such a position as that
is—quite—beneath your powers ?"

He turned his bright fair face to her with a

look of undisguised pleasure and amusement. "Oh no, mademoiselle," he said simply, "I could do nothing more : I am really no musician. So long as I can earn sufficient for my daily needs I am quite satisfied. This occupation leaves my days tolerably free; and I am of a curious turn; I want to learn a little about the life of the English artisan, and I learn a good deal about him here. But I am glad that you know now what I am and what I do; it was for Davy's sake alone, mademoiselle, that I presumed in the first instance to address you. I know very well that my position at the Parthenon would not have warranted such an intrusion."

"It was no intrusion : under the circumstances it was a duty," Vera said quickly.

He glanced at her suddenly, then looked down. There had been a curious dewy softness in those kindly eyes. "I thank you for saying so, mademoiselle," he answered.

The streets had become less narrow during the progress of their conversation. Vera lifted up her eyes and saw a wide space before her and the shining river Thames beyond. "The Embankment!" she exclaimed in some surprise.

“It is the nearest way,” said her companion. “But were you going to Piccadilly this afternoon. mademoiselle? Is it not a little late for your engagement there?”

“I suppose it is,” said Vera, ruefully consulting her watch. “Too late—I shall have to manage better another time. I will go to Kensington.”

“Yes, mademoiselle. And—we shall meet a cab presently, no doubt. Shall we walk upon that other side and enjoy a little of the freshness and the sunshine?”

Vera consented. They sauntered leisurely along the broad pavement. The fitful April sunshine cast flying gleams upon the flying water: a slight haze hung over the banks and bridges and distant towers of Westminster. A girl came up with violets for sale, but Vera was forced to shake her head: she had no money with her. Mr. Guyon noticed that her eyes lingered on the blue and white bunches; he turned and bought a couple.

“One I am going to take to Davy,” he said. as if to preface his request. “May I offer the other one to you, mademoiselle?”

Vera took the sweet, stiff little green-leaved bunch with a word of thanks, and raised it to her face. "It is very sweet. I love violets."

"They are my favourite flowers," said he, raising the other bunch as she had done. "But what a pity to tie them up so tightly with thick string, and to cut all the leaves after one pattern, too. Mademoiselle, it seems to me, I assure you, almost a sin to disfigure leaves and flowers after this fashion! Why do they not sell your sweet English violets as they come straight from the woods and fields? — loose, wet, fragrant, and natural!"

"We are in London," she answered, smiling.

"Is there nothing sweet and natural in London? I cannot believe that. I must try your flower-market—your Covent Garden, is it not?—perhaps I shall there be more fortunate. Do you like Russian violets too, mademoiselle?"

"Not quite so well as English ones, I am afraid. I suppose that you like them better?"

"Why should you think so, mademoiselle, if I may ask before replying?"

"I may be wrong," said Vera in some little

confusion, "but I had made up my mind that you were yourself a Russian——"

"And therefore that I must like Russian violets? I think, like you, that I like English ones best. And to satisfy my curiosity again, mademoiselle—I told you that I was of a curious disposition—may I ask why you have decided on my nationality?"

"You spoke just now of kopecks: that was all."

"Ah, did I?" Her companion turned away his face and seemed to hesitate for a moment; but resumed presently with all his usual lightness of tone: "You were quite right. I am a Russian, and in exile. I will go further and acknowledge that Guyon is only a Christian name and not a family one. You have penetrated further into my secret, mademoiselle, than Davy has done during all these months!" His voice showed some amusement—a fact which rather displeased Mademoiselle de Lusignan.

"I had no intention of penetrating any secret, Mr. Guyon. But I am interested in Russians and anything belonging to Russia, because of an old association that I have. I was called after a Russian lady—whose name I do not know."

Mr. Guyon looked round quickly. "Indeed? I noticed that you bore one of our favourite names. My mother's name was Vera," he added in a lower voice.

"I am sure that I have excited your curiosity now," she said, smiling.

"I confess it," he answered, with a slight bend of his head. "You must forgive me, mademoiselle; I was wondering who might be the countrywoman of my own whose name you bear, and whether I could help you to find her out, supposing that you wished to find her. But, no doubt——"

"I will tell you the whole story," she said, as he hesitated for a moment, "and you will see how it happened. My mother and father were in a French town—the town of Lusignan, from which I have taken my stage-name—when I was born. My father was a violinist; he had fallen into ill health and poverty, and my mother was nearly in despair, when a great Russian lady who had heard him play found out their distress, and came several times to help them. She held me in her arms during those visits, my mother told me, and said that I was like a little child whom she had lost, whose name was Vera; and she begged as a favour that I might be called Vera, and that she might be my godmother. She was of a Polish family, I believe, so she was of the Roman, not the Greek, Church. My father was a Roman Catholic also, and I was baptized in that Church, although I have lived as a Protestant ever since. But my parents died when I was so young that I forgot my sponsor's name; and she went back to Russia, no doubt, and soon forgot me."

Maurice Guyon did not speak. It seemed to Vera that his face was troubled by some new and strange emotion. It was with a very gentle manner that he turned to her at last, and said softly:

"Think rather, mademoiselle, that she remembered you to the last day of her life. Doubtless she would never forget that tie."

"I like to think that she is living," Vera replied, "and that some day I may meet her and thank her for her kindness to my mother."

Mr. Guyon's eyes dwelt on the girl with kindly interest.

"She would be surprised, no doubt," he said —and did Vera fancy only that he sighed ?—"to find the baby whom she had held in her arms grown into a woman of genius—a queen of song."

"Am I that indeed ?" she questioned slowly. "I think not yet."

"May I speak the truth, mademoiselle ?"

"If you will be so good."

"Well, then, let me say that your singing in Davy's room yesterday proved to me that of which I had been a little doubtful. You have genius, mademoiselle; genius and soul, and art beside. But you do not always sing in that way at your concerts, do you ? Am I unbearably impertinent, or do you think me right ?"

"You are right."

"I should think that it is the first time a bandsman ever presumed to criticise a well-known lady-singer in her own hearing," he said, half playfully, half seriously. "But courage ! I have seized my opportunity ; and the singer has too large a brain and heart to be offended by what I say. I think this then, mademoiselle : you have

a great career before you; you are young, and
you have time and power to perfect yourself, so
that you will take your proper place with the
greatest singers of our time.   You will have few
rivals, fewer equals; the world will be at your
feet.   Diva! I salute you!" He raised his hat
as he spoke, with a sparkle in his eyes, a slight
smile upon his lips. "And when all this comes
to pass, mademoiselle," he added, with a light
grace of manner which gave his words just the
right shade of meaning, just the emphasis which
kept them from growing either too serious or too
trivial, "I pray you remember the poor, starving
Russian violin-player, who had ears and eyes for
what was loveliest and best just five minutes
before the rest of the world perceived it."

He replaced his hat on his head with a smile
which was so frank and winning that Vera would
have felt herself churlish indeed to object either
to the criticism or to the compliment which accompanied it.

"I hope I may justify your expectations," she
said. "Whether I do or not, however, I shall
always have two great consolations: one, that I
am trying faithfully to interpret the music of the

great masters; and another, that I have always an outlet for what is strongest and wildest in me. When I am in trouble, I think I should go mad if I did not sing."

" You are happy, mademoiselle, to have that outlet."

Some graver shade upon his brow arrested Vera's answering words. Light-hearted as his manner seemed to be, there was something in the glance of his eyes, in a momentary expression of his face, that showed a depth of earnestness, even of sadness, behind the apparent gaiety. Indeed, when he was grave, his face fell naturally into something approaching melancholy of expression; the slightly-hollowed cheek, the finely-cut mouth and chin had a purity of outline that made him at times look almost stern. They walked on in silence, Vera's thoughts busy with his possible history; his, buried in the past.

The silence recalled Vera to a prosaic side of life. By the time that she reached home she felt sure that Mrs. Cradock would be awaiting her arrival in order to ring for their evening meal— high-tea at half-past five, before going to a concert-room, where she had an engagement that night. It behoved her to hasten back to Kensington.

" I see a cab standing empty," she said to Mr. Guyon. " I think that I must take it and go home. I am very much obliged to you for bringing me so far."

"Pardon me, the obligation is all upon my side. Is there anything more that I can do ? "

"Thank you, nothing."

He bowed after helping her into the cab, and would have retreated, but she held out her hand. He looked decidedly pleased as he took it in his own ; he even flushed up a little and seemed embarrassed. It struck Vera that he had been foolish enough to think that as he was, as he had said, " a starving violin-player" only, she would omit this customary mark of civility. He gave her a different explanation of his behaviour afterwards. Certainly, no such petty notion ever crossed his mind.

CHAPTER XI.

LUCY.

VERA's next visit to Davy took place on the following morning, and this time she did not come alone, but attended by Mrs. Cradock's maid. Just as the cab drove up to the door Mr. Guyon also arrived at it on foot. His face lighted up as he saw Vera; he lifted his hat and looked at her with a sort of eagerness and hurry that seemed like pleasure.

"Mademoiselle," he said, almost at once, " do you see that I have been successful ? There are sweet and fragrant and natural flowers to be had even in your city of gloom and smoke."

He carried in his hand a flat rush basket lined with wet moss and leaves, on which there lay, loose, long-stalked, and glistening with rain or dew, as if they had just been picked, a fragrant heap of sweet white violets.

"How lovely! how Davy will enjoy them!" said Vera, lifting her dark gray eyes earnestly to Mr. Guyon's face.

"Pardon me, mademoiselle," he said, as he showed her some other flowers in his hand, "these daffodils are Davy's favourites, and they are all for him; but the violets—if I may offer so small a gift—were for you, to show you what London can produce," he added, smiling.

"You are very kind, Mr. Guyon. They are sweet indeed."

"I will keep them for you until you go. They will be in your way just now."

"Thank you. But wait a moment." Vera separated two or three of the fragrant white blossoms from the others and fastened them into her brooch as she stood. "I shall have them all the morning now."

"That will help you not to forget them."

"You must think me very ungrateful," she said as she passed him to go upstairs.

"You *could* not be so, mademoiselle," he answered gravely. And something in his tone sent the colour to Vera's cheeks; so that she entered Davy's room with a face that caused him to tell her that she looked "like a rose in June."

"Which ain't your usual way, my pretty," he said, stroking her cheeks with his brown fore-finger; "for you're more like a white lily in general, or a white violet like them you've got there. Did Mr. Guyon give you those, dearie?" he asked, almost in a whisper.

"Yes, Davy."

"I thought so," said the old man, in a tone of inexpressible satisfaction. "He was off before daylight, with a young fellow that he's taken a fancy to—a tramp, I should call him—to a place miles out of London, where wild flowers grow. 'Where are you going?' I said to him. 'Don't be afraid, old man,' he answered me, 'I'll be back before noon; I'm going to get some white violets for a lady who is more like a white violet herself —so modest and white and sweet she is—than any woman I ever knew—except the mother that bare me.' And he said nothing more; but I knew what he meant, and I said to myself that you should know it too."

"A violet that blooms only to wither beneath

the gas lamps," Vera said softly, laying a burning face against his wrinkled hand.

"Always sweet, withered or not withered," he answered her; and no word of praise or compliment ever touched her more.

He lay still for a long time, and when he spoke again, she found out that he had grown perceptibly worse since she last saw him. He was restless and uneasy, and much disposed to talk. The nurse did not think, however, that the excitement of Vera's visit was bad for him, and she listened, therefore, without trying to silence him, while he spoke disconnectedly of her earlier years, of the Stangers and of her mother; also of some one whom she did not know, whose name was Lucy.

But after he had mentioned Lucy a change came over his face. The light leaped into his eyes, his lips trembled. He felt hurriedly under his pillow, and produced thence a little packet of discoloured papers, tied around with string.

"I had a dream last night," he said, holding the paper between his hands and nervously fingering the string. "I dreamt of Mr. Ravenscroft and you. I dreamt that he was coming back—— *You hope he will?*"

He put the question suddenly, in a terrible voice of anger and alarm. Vera started, but answered steadily enough.

"No, I hope not."

"I know you better. You want him to come and see you as you are now."

"Why should you speak to me of him, Davy?" she said, trying to quiet him as his voice grew fierce and his eyes wild. "I have almost forgotten him: forget him too."

"I must speak to you of him, missy. I have left you unwarned too long. It was your mother who came to me in my dreams last night and told me that she had trusted you to me and I had failed her. 'There is no one but you to tell her,' she said. 'No one but you. Make haste—make haste.'"

"Dear Davy, that was but a dream. Mr. Ravenscroft will never cross my path again. He helped me when I was a child; but everything is different now."

"Yes, now you are a woman and worth knowing; then you were a child. Besides, your mother told me to warn you," said Davy, with the strange commingling of prudence and of vagrant fancy which was often to be noticed in his speech. "I am to put you on your guard against him: I am to warn you, do you hear?"

Vera sighed assent. It was less easy to oppose him than to keep silence. He raised his finger and shook it imperiously in the direction of the nurse and Vera's maid, both of whom were in the room. "Tell them to go away," he said. "I don't want them: I want nobody but you."

Vera asked the two women if they could go into another room for a short time. She would call them if they were required. The nurse had a small apartment at her disposal: thither she led Janet, whilst Vera returned to Davy's bedside.

He lay back upon the pillows muttering to himself, with wandering eyes and pallid face; his fingers were busy with the string of his packet. Vera offered to untie it for him, but he only shook his head and fumbled at the knot. When it was undone, he fixed his wild eyes on her and addressed her solemnly.

"I wrote this paper, dearie," he said, "only a few months ago, although it is about matters that happened years before. My eyes are too dim, my voice is too weak, to read it to you now. Do you read it aloud to me that I may see whether it needs to be altered in any way. Sit where I can best see you, with your face to the light, and read slow; for I'm no scholar and can't follow if you read it fast."

He handed her two or three sheets of paper, written all over in a cramped but legible hand. Vera sat down, with her face to the light, as he had requested her to do, and began to read.

"This is the true narrative and testimony of me, David Rowe, written in the month of October 1877." So ran the opening sentence: further down the page the narrative itself began.

"I was born in the parish of Mickleham in Lincolnshire, though neither of my parents was Lincolnshire born. My father came of a Highland stock and my mother of a Romany tribe. It was from her that I got my knowledge of the stars and the way to read men's hands. She was skilful in herbs and roots, moreover, and used to be called 'The Wise Woman of Netherby.' My father died when I was young, and left me nothing but his fiddle and his love for music. Mother worked in the fields until I was old enough to go out and work for her.　Then I took to the shoemaking; and fiddled sometimes for pence at statute fairs and weddings and the like, and told folks' fortunes for a change——"

"If it's not written so correct as it should be, missy," interposed the writer, "take a pencil and put it straight.　I'm no scholar."

Vera nodded and resumed her reading.

"But my lameness prevented me seeing much of the villagers, and they were afraid of us both for our fierce, wild ways, and because, they said, we knew more than we ought to do.　But when I was close on twenty or thereabouts, mother one day brought home a baby girl whose parents had died of fever in the village, a tiny scared-looking little thing, as desolate as we were ourselves.　We could not bear to send her to the workhouse— she had such pretty ways with her—and she never was frightened either of mother or of me —I'm sure of that.　She grew up fair as the day and bright as the morning; and it was a sore thing for me when she said that she was old enough to earn her own living and would go and be maid to a fine widow-lady who was living half her time in Netherby and half in London.　Her name, which I take to be a foreign one, was Madame Waldstein——"

Here Vera came to a sudden stop and raised her eyes. "Yes," said Davy, with a fiery look from under his dark brows, " *you* know the name. *His* mother."

She dropped her eyes and went on with the reading.

"—— Madame Waldstein, who had been married before to a Mr. Ravenscroft, and was the mother of the squire of Netherby and his brother. I often saw these gentlemen : they were both fine, personable men. Philip and Gaston were their names. Philip, the elder, was a proud man and mean in his ways about money, but very careful that nobody should say ill of him. So he and his mother kept Mr. Gaston supplied with money, for Gaston had not a penny but what they gave him, and folks said he was kept very tight. Gaston was as proud as his brother, but open-handed and fiery, and he did not like the way he was treated, although he could not well complain for fear he should get less instead of more. I write all this down because it has to do, as I believe, with what came next.

"These young men's mother had married a foreign nobleman after old Mr. Ravenscroft's death; and when the Baron died she came back to England and lived at Ravenscroft Hall with her elder son. Mr. Philip had been married for a year or two when Lucy went to wait on Madame, I remember; and he had no children at first, so that people began to say that Gaston might come in for the estates after all. But he had a daughter afterwards.

"I was so fond of Lucy that I couldn't bear to see her going out to service. If I had been like other folks I should have asked her to marry me. But she would, perhaps, only have laughed at me, poor soul; so I said nothing. She went to the Baroness', and was very happy. Fine tales she told us of my lady, and of Mr. and Mrs. Philip, and of Mr. Gaston, who was always hanging about the house. But she soon stopped her tales. There were things that she would not tell. More than one was making love to her: and not of her own station. I heard of many—Captain Aylmer for one, and Mr. Gaston for another. Lucy was a beautiful girl, with hair like gold, and eyes as blue as the forget-me-nots that grew in the wet meadows.

"Lucy was there for a year and a half. Then suddenly she disappeared: nobody knew why. I saw Madame myself about her—an old lady dressed up in silks and jewels, who sat and smiled and smiled at me, and said that she knew nothing about the matter. She had had an illness, the old Baroness, and was weak and crippled, and she made that an excuse for doing nothing to help me in my search. She had an evil look in her eyes, too, which made me suspect her. Mark my words, whoever it is that reads this paper, she knew well enough what had become of Lucy. I would stake my life upon it that she knew!

"The Ravenscrofts were all away from home at the time when Lucy disappeared. If they had had a hand in it they concealed their work well. I found no trace of Lucy anywhere.

"It was then that I began to travel about with my violin—trying to find Lucy. In two or three years I allowed myself to join Jonas Stanger's company. I had given up the hope then of finding *her.*

"The lady that Stanger afterwards married used to play the piano for him at that time. She had a little girl, a strange frightened little thing, with a look about her of Lucy when first she came to my mother's house. Her hair was not so yellow, but it was soft as floss-silk—like Lucy's, and her skin had the milky whiteness of Lucy's too. That child was Lucy in her childhood over again to me."

"You must excuse the liberty, missy," said Davy apologetically. But Vera was touched by the comparison. She bent forward and laid her hand on Davy's as she read, while Davy turned his face away and plucked nervously at the bedclothes.

What Vera read need not be rehearsed. Davy had written down an account of the way in which he had found Lucy in the lane at Netherby, and of her subsequent death. He went on to speak of the little child, and of his own and his mother's aversion to it. And then he continued the story thus.

"My mother sent the child away," he had written. "It was a sweet pretty boy, with dark eyes like Lucy's own; and when I had gone back to Stanger's, after Lucy's funeral, I could not help but think of him and call myself a brute for letting Lucy's boy go to the workhouse. Yet I did nothing—nothing for weeks and months. It was only when the little girl that I had loved was taken away from me by Ravenscroft himself —it was always Ravenscroft as came between me and my happiness—it was only then that I made up my mind to go back to Netherby, to take Lucy's child out of the workhouse, and to behave to it as though it was my own. In this way I thought that I could make up for the cruelty that I had shown.

"I spoke to mother first. 'As you please,' says she. 'Don't bring the child to me; that's all. Mr. Hervey took it to the workhouse, and for aught I know it's in the workhouse still.'

"I went to the workhouse. But I did not find Lucy's child. I looked at every boy in the place, and I asked questions of every one that I thought likely to know anything about him— Timothy Worlaby, in especial, as was the porter of the place and remembered every child for forty years back—but I couldn't find any trace of him. There had been no boy called Bertie or

Moore, or any such name at all in Mickleham Workhouse.

"Mr. Hervey was in France at that time, and I could not ask him what he had done with the child. It's certain that he took the boy away from mother's cottage. Some months later I did manage to see him and I asked him about the boy. 'Oh, you're too late,' he said. 'The boy's relations took him away before his name was entered on the books.' 'Then he did go to Mickleham Workhouse?' I asked. 'I suppose so,' he said. But I don't believe him. I don't believe he ever took little Bertie to the workhouse. And I believe that he knows where the child is now and what became of him.

"I wish to leave to Lucy's child all the money that I possess. I live poorly, but I am not so poor as I seem. I have toiled and striven and saved for Lucy's boy. My savings are invested; the paper along with this one will show where. But I must find friends who will take charge of the money for Lucy's little son. To them I will commend him, and they shall have my savings in trust for him.

"I desire also to record the name of the man

who blighted my Lucy's life, broke her heart, and then deserted her. That man was Gaston Ravenscroft."

Here Davy's manuscript came abruptly to a close. Vera laid it down and looked at Davy with wistful anxious eyes. What more did he want? She had not long to wait.

"My dearie," he said at last, very tenderly, "my beauty, that would charm the heart out of a man with your sweet voice and your speaking eyes, will you remember what you have read? Don't let that man crush the life out of your body and your soul. Remember my warning, for God's sake."

"I will remember," Vera said. But, in spite of the evidence afforded by Davy's narrative, she could scarcely believe that Gaston Ravenscroft was the bad man that Davy represented him to be. She thought of the scene upon the Elmstone Downs, of the revolver that she herself had thrown down the fissure in the limestone rock. Did the story that she had heard afford an explanation of Gaston's agony?

She waited silently for Davy's next words.

But they were not addressed to her. He had fallen back upon his pillow; the energy had died out of his face and voice; his eyelids flickered and sank low.

“I’ve done it,” he muttered to himself. “I’ve warned her, Lucy. I shall not be afraid to see your face again. Nor Vera’s mother neither. I’ve done my best.”

His voice was hollow and feeble when he spoke again.

“I had a lawyer here a day or two agone,” he said. “He drew me up a will. Do you know what I’ve done, my darling? I’ve left my money to you and Mr. Guyon in trust for Lucy’s child. You’ll find the boy, won’t you? and give him the money from the man that loved his mother? Promise me that you’ll do that.”

“Yes, Davy. If Mr. Guyon consents I will.”

“He knows; he’ll consent. Call him in,” said Davy breathlessly. “He’s outside. I feel him near.”

Vera went somewhat doubtfully to the door, and, to her surprise, found that Maurice Guyon was at that moment ascending the narrow stair. Davy’s intuition had been correct. She beckoned the young man silently into the sick-room.

Maurice Guyon went to the musician's bed-side and took one of the brown and wrinkled hands between his own. "What is it?" he said softly. "What can I do?"

"*She* has promised to do all I wish," Davy answered. "You know what. Promise me, too; promise that you will find out Lucy's son. and I shall die happy."

Maurice Guyon stooped down and addressed his friend with singular gentleness. "Dear old man," he said, "you know so little of me! May I not, after all, be unworthy of your trust? You do not know me well enough for this."

Davy caught at the young, strong hand which rested so caressingly upon his own, turned it over, and with his trembling fingers traced the course of certain lines upon the palm. "Yes," he said, looking into Maurice's eyes with infinite placidity and trust, "I know: I know."

There was no more question of refusal. "I accept the trust," said the young man, with a tremor in his voice.

"I accept it too." said Vera clearly. They

exchanged a glance, and then their eyes fell somewhat confusedly. But Davy lay back upon his pillows with a look of infinite content.

From time to time, after this interview, Vera visited the old man, finding him at each visit weaker than when she saw him last. It became sadly evident that the end was very near.

"Davy," Vera whispered once when she heard him muttering, as he did constantly, the names of Lucy and Bertie and Gaston Ravenscroft,—"Davy, I am sure that Lucy forgives him now. Will not you also forgive him, as we all pray to be forgiven?"

"No," he muttered in a sullen and hopeless way; "I can't forgive him—and I won't. He ruined her—and me too—and I'll not—I can't —forgive him."

At last—it was on a Sunday afternoon—she found him unconscious. The grayness of death was already on his face. She sat beside him, with Maurice Guyon not far away, and waited silently and sadly for the hour of death.

They were both startled by and by to see a flicker of light in his dim eyes, to hear a murmur from those dying lips.

Vera bent down to listen. Painfully and slowly came the words; not all of them were intelligible.

"Lucy"—the well-loved name came first—"in the night—I dreamt she came—told me to forgive——" A confused murmur followed, then again more distinct utterances. "I am trying—I want to see her again. Pray for me; pray aloud."

This was no time for refusal. How could Vera have refused him? On her knees beside the bed she repeated the Lord's Prayer, pausing a little at one petition—"Forgive us our trespasses as we forgive those——"

"Ay," said the dying man, "that's it. Forgive us, as we forgive—as I forgive Ravenscroft——"

Then a great light came into his ashen face. He lifted up his hands and called "Lucy" in a tone of glad surprise. "Lucy," he said, "have you come back?"

Then, with his hands still lifted and his eyes turned to the bare, white-washed wall as if they saw beyond it and away, the old man died.

Maurice Guyon laid his hand upon Vera's hand and held it as he spoke.

"Come away, Vera; we can do nothing for him now."

And when she had kissed the dear dead face he led her from the room and took her home. She could never think of him as other than a friend when she recalled the sympathy and kindness that he had shown her in the hour of her grief.

It happened that Vera was obliged to sing at a great concert on the evening of Davy's funeral, at which she, together with Maurice, had been present. She had expected to find herself almost voiceless; but when the evening came a feverish excitement took possession of her, glowed in her cheeks, brightened her eyes, and gave strange power and sweetness to her voice. She sang as she had perhaps never sung before, and took the critical audience by storm.

Maurice Guyon had in some manner managed to gain admittance to the rooms set apart for the performers. Vera spoke to him once in the interval between the two parts of the concert.

"Am I singing well now?" she asked him.

" As well, do you think, as I sang once to *him* ?"
She was thinking still of Davy.

"Better, mademoiselle," he answered her.
" You are achieving a triumph."

It was in the very midst of this triumph,
whilst she was led forward to bow to an applauding crowd, that Vera suddenly caught sight of
the face of one of her hearers and saw in it the
face that had haunted her dreams for more than
half her lifetime—the face of the man to whom
she owed perhaps the whole success of her career
—the pale, proud, brooding face of Gaston
Ravenscroft.

PART III.—MAURICE.

CHAPTER XII.

WITH MADEMOISELLE DE LUSIGNAN.

GASTON RAVENSCROFT was in Asia Minor when Vera's letter was forwarded to him. He had been travelling in unfrequented places for many months, and had just arrived at the house of an old friend, who had long held the post of Consul in a small Oriental city. Vera's epistle therefore fell into his hands at a moment when he had no special project of travel or adventure in view, and he was able to give undivided attention to her communication.

It was a letter which vexed him exceedingly. He had almost forgotten the length of time that had elapsed since he left her at school in England, and was astonished, when he counted the years, to find that Vera must now be a young woman of two or three and twenty. He had vaguely meant to do something definite for her before this time; and he became very angry when he read Vera's assertion of her own independence. He was particularly displeased to hear that she had taken upon herself to return to England, and make engagements without waiting to hear from him: he certainly thought that she owed him so much consideration and respect. After fuming over the letter for a time, and talking about it to his friend, Charles Herbert, who furnished him with a pile of newspapers in which he found Vera's name many times repeated, and accompanied by terms of warmest praise, he made up his mind suddenly that he would return to England, and try once more to persuade Mr. Hervey to receive his granddaughter at Netherby. He had not much hope of success; but he was resolved that, if he failed in persuading Mr. Hervey, he would tell Vera the story of her mother's marriage, and let her make what use of the facts she chose.

When this decision was made he found that the prospect of treading English soil once more

was not disagreeable to him.   He had recovered
from the effects of his early sorrows; they were
indeed not forgotten, and they had left their
traces on his mind and on his character, but
they had naturally dwindled in importance since
the day when he very nearly put an end to his
existence upon Elmstone Downs. He had greatly
changed since then.

His friend Herbert travelled with him to
England. They went to London together, and
here one of the first objects that met Gaston's
eyes was an announcement that the celebrated
artiste, Mademoiselle de Lusignan, would sing
two songs at a concert in St. James' Hall that
evening.

"It cannot be little Vera!" he said laughingly
to Herbert. But he bought tickets for himself
and his friend, and went at eight o'clock to St.
James' Hall.

Vera had been very present to his mind
during the past few weeks—an insignificant-
looking little maiden, with fine eyes, and a voice
like a nightingale's—a wild, untamed, delicate
little thing of impulse, for whom he had imagined
that the life of a public singer would be unen-

durable. Yet, with the strong will and the power of self-control. which she had at times exhibited, he acknowledged to himself that if she had in truth submitted to the hard toil and training involved by success in her profession, she might possibly have developed into a rare and striking creature. He awaited Mademoiselle de Lusignan's first appearance therefore with great interest and curiosity ; but when she came he drew his eyebrows together with a look of perplexity and astonishment which Herbert, who was sitting beside him, noticed at once.

" It is not your *protégée*, then ? " he said.

" Upon my word I can't tell. I must wait and see."

He saw before him a fair and gracious woman, tall, slender, but exquisitely proportioned, with a mingled grace and dignity of mien which was singularly attractive. Of this peculiar grace there could be no doubt ; but Ravenscroft was not equally sure as to her beauty. The features of her face were delicate, but not strictly regular ; her complexion seemed to be fair—but how could he judge of her complexion ? Had rouge and enamel nothing to do with that dazzling red and white ? Was that mass of golden hair her own ? Did those marvellous eyes owe their brilliancy to artistic tinting of eyelashes and eyelids, and was the arched distinctness of the dark eyebrows due to nature or to a hair-pencil ?

She had one of those voices which are heard a few times in a lifetime only—a voice which would make her name of European reputation. Some faults in its management there might be still ; but it was wonderfully sweet, searching, and sympathetic. This young *artiste* had a great career open to her,—so much was plain to Ravenscroft from the very first,—and she sang as one inspired, not merely as she had been taught, but with a touch of that divine fire which we call genius. Never was the success that befell her that evening more thoroughly deserved. But it was not until the very close of the performance that Gaston Ravenscroft could decide whether she was " his Vera " or a stranger.

It was at the last moment, while he was still studying her with baffled wondering eyes, that her eyes rested upon him in turn. She started ; he fancied that she turned pale, and that her lips for a moment lost their smile ; then, still looking him full in the face, she deliberately bowed—yes, to him and himself only. After that first moment she showed no outward trace of confusion or embarrassment; yet she had recognised him, and Ravenscroft seemed more moved by the fact than she. He turned to Herbert with visible excitement of manner. " It is my Vera," he said, "and she knew me. Did you see her, Herbert? She knew me again— poor little soul!" and he laughed rather unsteadily as he spoke.

" Yes, she knew you," said Herbert, becoming gravely observant of his friend. " You are probably less changed than she would be. What are you doing now?"

For Mr. Ravenscroft, with a half smile and a determined air, was writing upon one of his own visiting-cards. " I'll have her address, at any rate," he said. " So she thought to cast me off entirely, did she? I fancy I can make her feel my guardianship still."

" What are you going to do?"

Ravenscroft showed the writing. " Will Mademoiselle de Lusignan allow an old acquaintance to have the honour of calling upon her ?—G.R." He rose while Herbert was reading it.

"Satire is a dangerous weapon with a woman of that kind," said Herbert, simply returning him the card.

"Why should she take it as satire? Wait a minute: I must find some means of conveying this to her."

The means were found, though not very easily; and then Ravenscroft insisted upon waiting some minutes near the door to see whether any present notice would be taken of his communication. They seemed to be waiting in vain, however, and were just turning away when Ravenscroft heard himself addressed by name.

"Mr. Ravenscroft, I think?"

Gaston turned eagerly. A young man with a note in his hand stood before him, bowed, and spoke.

"Mademoiselle de Lusignan desired me, if possible, to find you and to give you this note. If there is any answer I can take it to her if you will allow me to do so."

Gaston opened the note in silence. Herbert

meanwhile observed the messenger with some keenness : a handsome man, apparently about six or seven-and-twenty, with fine features and a long fair moustache : not in evening dress—in fact decidedly out at elbows, but with the manners and bearing of a gentleman. Such, at least, would have been Herbert's verdict.

These were the words read by Gaston Ravenscroft :

"Vera de Lusignan thanks Mr. Ravenscroft for his kind remembrance of her. She will be happy to see Mr. Ravenscroft at any time between twelve and five which may suit him best, upon any day this week. Perhaps Mr. Ravenscroft will kindly let her hear when she may expect him."

An address was given below.

"Is Mademoiselle de Lusignan still here?"

"She is, sir."

"I might give her my answer by word of mouth then ?"

"Pardon : Mademoiselle de Lusignan will see nobody to-night."

"May I know to whom I am speaking?" said Ravenscroft with ironical courtesy.

The young man's face changed. It coloured a little and his eyes flashed. But he controlled himself, and answered with coolness and gravity :

"For the present I am Mademoiselle de Lusignan's messenger."

"I will not trouble you," said Ravenscroft dryly.

Mademoiselle de Lusignan's messenger lifted his eyebrows a little, gave the speaker a searching glance out of a pair of very keen blue eyes, then bent his head in token of comprehension and retired. Gaston watched him out of sight, before turning upon his heel, with a haughty exclamation to Herbert :

"Who is *that* fellow, I should like to know ?"

"An admirer, probably."

"Insolent puppy!"

"I have seen him before," said Herbert reflectively, "or somebody very like him. I wonder where."

Ravenscroft went to his hotel and thence wrote a note to the address given, fixing his visit for the following afternoon. He sallied forth at the appointed time with an odd feeling that he was about to meet the child whom he had befriended twelve years before, and not the beautiful vision seen upon the performers' platform in a public hall. But in truth he met neither.

The house in which Vera and Mrs. Cradock had taken rooms stood back from the road, and was fronted by a pretty little garden, bright with roses and geraniums. As Ravenscroft went up the path from the little iron gate, the front door opened to let out an earlier visitor. For a moment Gaston was more startled than he would have liked to confess: the visitor was the young man who had given him Vera's note on the previous evening. He was intimate, then, with Mademoiselle de Lusignan? The eyes of the two men met with a certain expression of hostility, but they passed each other without any other sign of recognition. It was with no well-pleased look upon his face that Gaston Ravenscroft knocked at Vera's door.

The clock was striking four as the neat maid admitted him to a pretty little sitting room, till then unoccupied, and left him there alone. Ravenscroft looked round him. The sound of a monotonous voice reading aloud had struck upon his ear. On his right hand the entrance to another room was screened by a portière ; but the portière had been slightly disturbed and afforded him a glimpse of an interior which instantly riveted his attention.

He saw a pleasant room, softly shaded from the sun and bright with flowers. A gray-haired, sensible-faced, elderly lady in black silk sat in an arm-chair reading aloud. On a *chaise longue* lay Vera de Lusignan at full length, with her arms crossed behind her head.

Was it done for effect ? Gaston wondered cynically. The attitude was one of repose, almost of indolence, and yet of wonderful grace. She looked singularly slight and young in this position ; and her soft white dress was of almost childish simplicity. Her only ornament was a bunch of violets which she had fastened into the bosom of her dress.

" I should have known her if I had seen her thus at first," said Gaston to himself as he stood unseen, and looked.

The flush that her face had worn whilst she was singing had gone, but she was lovely with the loveliness of extreme refinement and delicacy. Her complexion was very fair, and her skin had a peculiar whiteness—not the dead whiteness of ill health, but a pearly transparency and freedom from spot or blemish, which was very striking. The fair hair was drawn back from her forehead, but the shorter hairs refused to lie smooth, and clustered above her low broad forehead in a perfect halo of tiny natural curls. Her eyebrows were so dark and well defined as to afford a strong contrast to the fair hair and complexion; the long eyelashes were also dark, and the beautifully shaped eyes were of a pure gray that looked almost black in shadow. Though intellect and will predominated over feeling in her face, with its strongly developed brow and chin, yet at first sight, to unobservant eyes, the extreme fairness of her skin gave an effect of fragility, and the infantine sweetness of eye and lip an impression of great pliability of disposition.

Ravenscroft heard his name announced by the maid and hastily turned his face away from the opening. In another instant the sound of sweeping garments was heard, the rings of the curtain rattled as it was drawn aside, and Vera herself stood before him. She shook hands with him simply, and did not say much : her manner struck him as gentle, cold, and even a trifle inanimate. He might have supposed her tame and spiritless if he had not heard her sing the night before.

She conducted him into the next room, where the gray-haired lady was still sitting. "You may perhaps remember Mrs. Cradock?" she said. "You had some correspondence with her at one time. She has been a very kind friend to me."

Ravenscroft found it less embarrassing to exchange a few sentences with Mrs. Cradock than to pursue a conversation with Vera, who meanwhile rang the bell for tea, and then stood silent for some minutes, apparently engaged in collecting the loose sheets of music upon an open piano. To Gaston's eyes she was perfectly calm. Mrs. Cradock, who knew her better, saw from the faint rose-tinting of her cheeks and the slight restlessness of her movements that she was unusually agitated. Presently Ravenscroft rose and offered her a chair. This brought her to a seat between him and Mrs. Cradock, where he could see her face and address an occasional remark to her. He wanted to make her talk; but she was so still, so frozen, either by pride or shyness, that she became more of an enigma to him than ever. Afternoon tea proved a diversion. Vera seemed more at ease behind the tray, and Ravenscroft watched her with a sort of surprise as her slim white fingers moved quickly amongst the pretty shallow cups and saucers. He began to see that she was embarrassed, but that embarrassment failed to make her awkward—only silent.

Mrs. Cradock felt her presence to be an oppression, and slipped away as soon as she had sipped her tea, in spite of Vera's piteous glance. Mr. Ravenscroft was glad to see her go; but he wondered a little how to introduce the subject of Vera's prospects in talking to her alone. This fair, still girl was difficult to treat as the baby he had thought her. And she seemed inclined to give him no opening for conversation on any but the most indifferent topics.

But he was wrong. After a few careless remarks, and one or two long pauses, Vera turned to him with a sudden change of attitude and countenance. She clasped her slender hands together upon her lap and crimsoned to her temples as she spoke.

“Mr. Ravenscroft, I hope you did not think me ungrateful when I ventured to act for myself. You were very far away, and my friends said that I ought not to wait.”

The answer that she expected did not immediately follow. She looked up at him pleadingly, and made some silent subtle comments on his face and the changes that she saw therein. Freed from the hairy growth which he had cultivated in Asia Minor, with the exception of a dark moustache, browned by many an Eastern sun, far sterner and harder in expression than it had been twelve years before, his face struck Vera at that moment with a sudden sense of surprise at its massiveness and power. It was still a handsome face, with fine bold lines, but there was a certain grimness about the strong contour of brow and chin, a latent fire in the glance of those deep-set brilliant eyes, an ominous knitting of the dark eyebrows, which promised neither patience, humility, nor good-humour, and were far more imposing than amiable. Vera looked at him, thought that her defence had sounded weak, yet felt more courageous now that the subject had been broached than she had done before.

The reply, when it came, was abrupt and ungracious enough. "And what if I do think you ungrateful? It does not signify to you now; you are successful, and that is all you want."

"Not all."

"What else do you require?"—sarcastically.

"I should be glad to have the esteem and—and—affection"—the word trembled upon her lips for a second or two before she uttered it—"of my friends."

Gaston looked at her with an ironical smile.

"Verily you ask much, Mademoiselle de Lusignan! And who may your 'friends' be? You had not too many when I saw you last. What friends have you had who counselled you not to wait?"

Her face turned pale and her eyes looked grieved and puzzled, but she answered with a patient simplicity which was not without its pathos.

"God has been very good to me. He has given me a great many friends. I owe them a great deal—more than ever I can repay," she added, with a melting of her gravity into a bright, sweet look which directed the application of her words to himself. "But, ah! I forgot; you do not like to hear of repayment or of thanks."

Gaston bit his lip, and felt the shock of something very like unpleasant surprise at the tone of her first sentence. "Dévote!" he said to himself, "I should not have thought it. Where did I hear that story of some great singer who never went on the stage without praying that she might do her part well? Vera seems to be moving on the same lines."

"I like gratitude," he said aloud, coldly.

"And you think I have not been grateful?" —again with the sensitive flushing from brow to chin.

"I did not mean to say that. But of course the fact remains," said Ravenscroft dryly, "that you have preferred the advice of other friends to mine; and although I never wanted to force mine upon you, I think it would have been better for you if you had consulted me before taking so important a step in life as leaving the school where you had been placed, in order to teach and to sing in public. You did not do me that honour, and I do not wish to claim a right to it.

You informed me of your *decision* only : it was very kind of you to do so, I am sure, but, under the circumstances, unnecessary. I could hardly have expected you to await my opinion."

" Could I have had your opinion in less than six or eight months ? "

" Would six or eight months have been so serious a loss to you at your age ? Six months more study,—I had the Conservatoire at Milan in my mind if your voice were worth it, as it is, though your style is not faultless yet, Mademoiselle de Lusignan,—and then you could have come out under better auspices than those which you have secured for yourself."

Vera writhed under the lash of his keen tongue, but ventured to oppose his dictum. " I had good introductions. It was considered that these concerts at St. James' Hall would give me an excellent chance. I was engaged for the season," she said.

" Of course. Oh, doubtless the end justified the means. You are very successful ; and as I, being an unsuccessful man, worship success, I congratulate you on the measure of it that you have gained."

But Vera's cup was full. He had taunted her until she could bear no more. She answered him as vehemently as ever she had answered Jonas Stanger and her daughters in the days of her passionate childhood; and he was not displeased to have provoked the outburst.

"It is not true; it is not true," she said. "I care nothing for the success except for its making me free and independent—is it that which you dislike? You forget how you repulsed me when I once ventured to thank you in a letter for your kindness, and how you refused to give me any advice at all when at Rosenthal I asked what profession you wished me to adopt! 'Decide for yourself: I do not wish you to consult me,' you said then. Was that answer of yours no reason for my acting as I did? Was I not justified?"

He had risen from his seat and stood with his shoulder against the mantelpiece, with his eyes studiously averted from her face, but he was silent. She continued passionately:

"Indeed, indeed, I was not ungrateful! But I was half afraid to write to you at all, when you had so sternly forbidden me to do so! How

could I know that you cared about my prospects ?
I thought that you would be glad to have me
off your hands : you gave me every reason to
think so.”

“ No, Vera.”

“ But I was obliged to think so : you made
me think so,” said the girl, standing before him,
so that in spite of himself he was obliged to see
the quivering lips and indignant eyes, and to
hear the quick breaths that tore up the sentences
almost with sobs. “ I would have given anything—done anything—for you when I was a
child : you might have taken the whole management of my life if you had chosen. But you
refused to do anything but give me money. Oh,
it was good, it was kind, of you to do that, but
is money everything ? You told me that you
would have nothing to do with *me*. From that
moment I could not—I *could* not feel as if your
gifts were anything but burdens. Ah, yes, I
was ungrateful : I see it now. But *you* made it
hard ! ”

“ Yes, ” said Ravenscroft in an odd tone, “ I
did. I thought I was right.”

“ But now ? ”

“Now,” he said, looking at her face with a mixture of shame and hardihood which she did not understand, “ now I wish I had left myself the right to reproach you.”

“You acknowledge that you have not?” she asked, in utter astonishment at this sudden change of tone.

“ I acknowledge it.   I was unjust.”

“ And you see,” she said tremblingly, “ that I would gladly have consulted you if I had known that I might ?—that it was your own doing ?”

A pause ensued before he said “ Yes.”

She drew a long breath. “ I am glad,” she said, sitting down and covering her face.   “ I could not bear that you should think me so ungrateful !”   And for some minutes her tears flowed silently but fast.

There was a long silence.   Ravenscroft moved up and down the room, glanced perplexedly at the fair bowed head, and finally came and stood before her.

“ I don’t think you are much tamer than you used to be, Vera,” he said lightly.   “ You fire up precisely as you did when I saw you last.   But you were more forgiving then, child—I beg your pardon : I suppose I ought to say Mademoiselle de Lusignan, like all the rest of the world."

This drew her head up. She looked at him with a great radiance in her beautiful eyes. "Do you mean to be only like all the rest of the world to me ? " she said ; " or what you were in my childhood—my best and kindest friend ? "

A new and sudden consciousness of her womanly charm, of the sweetness of her eyes, the grace of her manner, made Gaston Ravenscroft falter in his answer.

" Your friend, Vera," he said at last in a softened tone. " Now and always your true and faithful friend—if neither the kindest nor the best."

CHAPTER XIII.

MAURICE'S PLAN.

VERA had no occasion to tell Mr. Ravenscroft that Maurice Guyon had never visited her before that afternoon when the two men met almost at her door. There had been no appointment between them; it had simply occurred to Maurice that he would take to her the violin that Davy had wished her to possess, and that, if she wanted to consult him respecting Davy's legacy to the missing child, she would then have the opportunity of doing so.

He was shown at once into the little sitting-room, whither Vera came to meet him. She seemed at once to understand his errand.

"Davy's violin?" she said quickly.

"It was a trust committed to me, mademoiselle," Maurice Guyon answered. "Davy wished you to have the instrument on which, as a child, he said you had often longed to play."

Vera said "Thank you" in a low tone; then moved to the table and opened the case that stood upon it. On seeing the violin, she laid her hand upon it gently and let it linger there, as if she would have caressed it for the sake of its former owner. There seemed to Maurice something very tender and beautiful in this action, something very lovely in the silence with which she looked upon this memorial of the dead. For he had seen enough of Vera to be aware that her silence covered deep reserves of feeling, and that her pale cheek and lowered eyes indicated more emotion than another woman's burst of tears. He honoured her for her self-control, and waited until she herself should break the silence.

"I have written to his mother," at last she said, without lifting her eyes.

"Ah?"—— He looked at her inquiringly.

"She sent a few lines in reply. She wishes for no help; she did not seem to grieve for her son's death. He had been long dead, she said, to her. How strange it is," said Vera, taking her hand off the violin, and moving away from the table a few steps, "that persons can be dead to each other in this life! It is very sad."

A flash of fiery meaning seemed to shoot across the young man's face, and then to leave it colder and darker than it had been before. "Sad it is, no doubt, mademoiselle," he said softly; "but strange? It is too frequent to be strange."

Vera stopped short in her gentle movement across the room; he could not but notice the sudden stillness of her slim straight figure and the averting of her graceful head. His words had touched her now, as hers had touched him before.

"I suppose you are right. I know that there are persons to whom I, for instance, have died, although I formed part of their lives once. But people do not let this happen knowingly; they do not often cast a person away from them and say, 'You are henceforward dead to me.' They merely let old friends slip, and then some day we wake up to find we are nothing any longer to those who have been all the world to us."

She spoke almost with indignation, and yet

there was a speculative melancholy in her tone which made her hearer doubt whether she were quoting from her own experience or not. He smiled with quiet, covert irony.

" *You* would not cast off an old friend wittingly ; I am sure of that, of course, after seeing what I have seen ; but others—other women—act differently. An old friend ?—an old glove : it can be taken off or put on at pleasure, or thrown away. A breath of adversity, suspicion, disgrace, blights a friendship as an east wind blights a rosebud."

She turned round and let her clear dark gray eyes dwell upon him reflectively, with a certain amount of pity and inquiry reflected in their translucent depths, before she said—

" We have all different kinds of experience. I have known examples of strong friendship and great faithfulness ; perhaps you have met with examples on the other side, and judge every one by them."

He laughed carelessly, but his face flushed a little as he answered.

" You think me easily influenced, Mademoiselle. I would not presume to contradict you, but, with your permission, I will tell you the story of a friend of mine—a story which will not occupy much time in telling, but which will serve to illustrate my point."

"Pray tell it me," said Vera. "Will you not sit down? I am afraid that I have kept you standing all this time; it is because I am so restless to-day; I feel as if I must walk up and down the room. But I will sit still now."

"Do not let me tire you," said Maurice gently. "Shall I go away now and tell you my little story another time? After all, it is not worth telling."

"I want to hear it," she said, seating herself and turning her face to him. "Please go on."

He was silent for a few moments, as if collecting his thoughts. Then he turned away from her a little, and spoke slowly, with his eyes bent on the floor.

"Mademoiselle, I had a friend once—in St. Petersburg—a man who longed, like myself, for freedom of thought and action in Russia such as you have here in England. He did not conspire against the Czar's life, but he did sympathise with the men who were spending time, and energy, and money, and brains upon the one object of their lives—the propaganda of what they thought to be the truth. He himself helped them in this object, and, when some of his friends were in danger, he hid them in his house. He was betrayed to the police,—by whom he never knew,—his house was searched, the *suspects* found and arrested. The police were brutal and violent; my friend struck one of them to the ground, and seriously, though accidentally, injured him. For these offences, he was first condemned to death, and then to perpetual exile in the mines of Siberia."

"How terribly unjust! Could nothing be done to save him?"

Maurice shook his head.

"He was betrothed, mademoiselle, to a lady —young, rich, beautiful; he loved her, and he thought that she loved him. When he was condemned, his one thought was this: '*She* will be faithful to me throughout. *She* will be my wife, and come with me even to Siberia.' For such things have happened before: other women have followed the men they loved into exile; was

she, whom he believed to be the pearl of woman-
hood, to be less true than they?"

"No, oh no!" said Vera, as if he had ap-
pealed to her for an answer to the question. The
story had carried her completely with it; her
eyes were shining, her lips parted, with interest
and expectation. "Oh no, there could be no
doubt. Of course she went with him."

The young man turned a nervous twitch of
his mouth into a smile.

"You are mistaken, mademoiselle. She
would not even see him again. She sent him
no farewell. Before six months had passed she
had married a kinsman of his own—the man
upon whom his estates had been conferred by
Imperial command."

"All women would not have been so false," said
Vera indignantly. "You do not think so? You
have not lost faith in them, because one woman
was faithless—*to your friend?*" She said the last
words with some emphasis, and gave him one keen
glance as she did so. But he did not look up.

"No, mademoiselle, I have not lost faith in
all. I thought I had, but I find I was
mistaken."

"And your friend?" said Vera hastily. "He went to Siberia?"

"Mademoiselle, yes."

"But he was pardoned afterwards? It was such a small offence! It was a virtue—not a crime!"

"He was not pardoned."

"But he escaped?"

"Do men escape from Siberia?" said the young man slowly, as if weighing all his words.

"Why, yes, sometimes."

"That is true. Bakunin, the Nihilist, escaped about the year 1860. He got on board an American ship at Novo-Nikolaievsk, and went first to Japan and then to North America."

"And your friend——"

"Another time, mademoiselle—pardon me—I will tell you all about my friend another time."

His voice was husky, and it seemed to Vera as if his eyes had grown wet with tears. He screened them with his hand for a few moments—silently, but with nothing of an Englishman's proud reserve. He showed his emotion openly and simply, knowing that it was not a thing of which to be ashamed. Vera held her peace;

she was sure already that the story which he
had told her was his own.

Vera was silent out of sympathy, but not
because she would have feared, even after his
prohibition, to question him. She had begun
dreamily to wonder whether it were possible that
she and Maurice had been friends or kindred
in another state of existence. There are persons
who seem to us, even at a first meeting, like old
acquaintances, whom accident alone has hitherto
kept away. So with Maurice and Vera. They
had never been strangers from the moment when
they first stood together at Davy's dying bed.

"Thank you, mademoiselle," he said at last;
though Vera did not know why he should thank
her, and indeed he scarcely knew himself. "Let
me now fulfil the rest of my commission. I
have some papers to place in your hands. I fear
that I am detaining you too long."

"Not at all, Mr. Guyon. Ah, Davy's
papers—— You read them?"

She asked the question with some timidity.

"I read them, mademoiselle."

"And what," said Vera slowly, "what do you
think that we had better do?"

The papers were laid upon the table at her side. She took them up, and turned them slowly in her hands as she spoke. Maurice watched her rather anxiously.

"Have you anything to propose, mademoiselle?" he asked her.

She raised her candid eyes and fixed them upon his face. "Mr. Guyon," she said, "I will tell you exactly what I feel. Mr. Ravenscroft is coming to see me this afternoon. When he speaks to me I shall half expect to hear him say: 'What is it that you have heard of me? What secret of mine do you hold that I do not know?' And I shall feel that I am mean and dishonourable in knowing what I do. What I propose is that we should hand the papers over to Mr. Ravenscroft and say to him : 'These concern you. Take them and find for yourself the son that you thought you had lost.' I wish to tell him all."

"Then *you*," said Maurice with emphasis, "*you* have more faith in Gaston Ravenscroft than Davy had?"

"Far more," she answered steadily.

"You think that Mr. Ravenscroft would rejoice to hear of Davy's suppositions? For we have not the slightest evidence to go upon. If we had, it would be a very different matter. What have we to tell him?"

Vera was silent.

"Give me a few days' grace, at least, mademoiselle," said Maurice in his winning voice. "I should like to go down to Netherby and see Davy's mother, and try to trace the child who was sent to the workhouse. If I am unsuccessful there, I will come back; then we can try your plan. It is quite possible that Mr. Ravenscroft knows something of the matter already."

Vera did not agree with Maurice's judgment. Still she yielded the point; there was a certain pleasure in yielding a point to Maurice Guyon.

"I will do just as you think best, Mr. Guyon. If you fail—if you hear nothing—then perhaps we can devise another plan. It is very good of you to take this trouble."

"Did you not think that I would take trouble for my friends, mademoiselle?"

"I am sure that you would—for Davy."

"Yes—for Davy; and—may I not say it?—

for you as well.   I may think that I am working for you too, may I not ?"

She hesitated.   " If it pleases you to think so——" she said at last.   She left the sentence incomplete, but it was plain that she had granted the request.

" Will you think me presumptuous for suggesting one thing ? " she said, after a short pause, which to her was instinct with happy meaning. " Your engagement at the Parthenon——"

" I will leave it."

" But—can you ?   Ought you ? "

" Mademoiselle," said the young man, with a bright look of determination on his face, " I can do for another what I did not care to do for myself.   You will call me perverse if I tell you that I have worked for myself rather because I chose than because I need.   If I spoke a word, if I lifted a finger, I could get sufficient for all my wants.   So you need not think that I am resigning much when I resign my few shillings a week at the Parthenon."

" Perhaps," said Vera, " you are resigning something more—some plan of your own—some freedom or independence——"

" Say rather some foolish pride, mademoiselle," he answered gravely. "It is not much that I shall gain, to be sure—a pittance only ; but it is there for me if I put out my hand. I have been intending to claim it for some time."

" Don't make any sacrifice, Mr. Guyon," said Vera, the quick colour rising in her fair cheeks. "You are acting for others, not for yourself. You ought to have no expense in the matter. I——"

And there she stopped short, for Maurice Guyon's face and gesture entreated silence.

"May I not do something for Davy too ? Do you want to keep to yourself all the pleasure of giving, mademoiselle ?" he said in a tone of gentle remonstrance. " I assure you," he added more earnestly, " I am doing nothing but what it is right for me to do. I have hitherto neglected to put myself into communication with certain friends of mine, because I fancied that they did not trust me as I had expected them to do. It may have been a foolish fancy; at any rate, I will go to them at once. They were very kind to me as a boy ; I think they will be kind still."

"But must you ask them for any anything? Could you not ask me as easily? It is for Davy's sake!"

"Dear mademoiselle," said Maurice, almost tenderly, "I shall ask them only for *my own.* I shall need nothing more."

"I understand. I beg your pardon for my mistake."

"There is no need; I did not explain myself sufficiently. I will go at once," said Maurice with some eagerness, "and then I shall be ready to start for Netherby as soon as I am free from the Parthenon business. Mademoiselle, I thank you for your great kindness."

But although he announced his intention so energetically, he seemed to find it hard to tear himself away. The papers were slowly gathered up, with a word or two between each; reluctantly at last he took his leave, after a lingering pressure of the slender fingers that were silently held out to meet his own, and a word of farewell which was in itself a pledge of swift return.

He left the house, and found himself face to face with Gaston Ravenscroft at Vera's door.

CHAPTER XIV.

VERA'S FRIENDS.

IF Gaston Ravenscroft had thought seriously over his first conversation with Vera, and the words and acts immediately preceding it, he might have found occasion to accuse himself of great inconsistency. But he was not a man who reflected much on his own actions. He was always said to be a man of strong will. Perhaps it was only an obstinate one. It certainly was apt at times to veer from one point to another with suddenness proportioned to the violence of his disposition. Never of a very tractable nature, he had now for many years accustomed himself to look upon his own wishes and emotions as the sole limits to his will and the only laws that he acknowledged. This tendency, moreover, had been increased by an adventurous life of exploration, such as suited

his tastes and habits better, he used to say, than
the humdrum existence of an English squire.
Above all a man of whims, crotchets, and eccen-
tricities, he had seldom shown himself more
whimsical than in his dealings with Vera Marlitt.
As a child, he had petted her; as a young girl,
he had liberally provided for her welfare, but
refused to enter into any personal relation with
her, expressly declining to take advantage of the
authority that he might have claimed; yet when
his *amour-propre* had been wounded by her
independent stand, he had at once hurried back
to England in order to assert the binding nature
of a tie which he had taken the utmost trouble
to sever! So far all was bad: he was acting with
the impulsive selfishness of a man who had done
a kind action for the sake of his own pleasure
rather than the benefit of the recipient; and yet
there was a better motive at work within him
than he chose to show. His very desire to provide for Vera's future made him dislike her acting
independently of him: the fear that she might
have cast away her chances and injured her own
prospects brought him to England on her account.
He had forgotten that she was a woman grown,

and he was of course guilty of culpable negligence in forgetting it, but it was not unaccountable negligence in a man who had renounced his own home ties, and believed himself bound by no duties.　He had long ceased to care for anything but how best to seize and enjoy the fleeting moment; he had no aims and no ambitions.　It was perfectly characteristic of him that at a moment of intense wretchedness he should have tried to put an end to his own life.　He thought it the most natural thing in the world for a man to take the only means in his power of ridding himself of torture as soon as it became excessive. His want of patience, and in some cases of fortitude, had been a marked feature with him from boyhood.　Physically he could dare and endure anything; it was in the moral region that he failed.

Yet Gaston Ravenscroft had qualities that merited esteem.　He was generous; he was tender-hearted to the weak and poor; he had a great scorn for the meaner vices of humanity, for anything that savoured of truckling, cowardice, niggardliness, or deceit.　His own faults inclined to the opposite extreme—to lavishness, rashness,

outspoken arrogance, and pride. He was a man
of rare gifts, who had chosen to fling them wan-
tonly away because he disdained the importance
that they would give him in the eyes of the
vulgar crowd.

Vera de Lusignan, in meditating upon this
strangely undisciplined nature, surmised that it
had received some terrible shock before it was
fully developed, either for good or evil; that there
had been some tremendous convulsion, as of the
rending of rocks and letting loose of the elements
in a mighty volcanic eruption; and that he
would bear the traces of this struggle to his dying
day. She called to mind the influences of his
earlier years; she remembered the cynicism and
worldliness of his mother; and she came to a
dangerous conclusion—for a woman in what
concerns a man—that circumstances had been
greatly against him, and that, though not wholly
free from blame, he was more sinned against
than sinning!

Another inconsistency made itself manifest in
that first interview with Vera. He had meant
to show himself ready to be her friend, and yet
he could not refrain from upbraiding her (un-

justly as he knew) for ingratitude. He would
not have spoken in this manner, he told himself
afterwards, if she had not angered him by her
cold demeanour and by the appearance of that
handsome stranger at her door. (How she was
responsible for his appearance Gaston did not
inquire of himself, and was not likely to ascertain.) Certainly he had allowed his vexation to
get the better of his reason. And then she had
fought him gallantly,—he admired her for her
resistance,—and had forced him to admit that he
had been unjust. He had yielded unwillingly
and in dudgeon at the time; but he had known
that she was right.

He came away from the house with a certain
excitement and exhilaration of feeling that proved
him to be younger at heart than he would have
cared to acknowledge; and all through the evening he was conscious of a glow of interest and
animation to which he had long been a stranger.
"The little witch!" he said to himself, as he
remembered the sweet eyes and silver-keyed
utterance, which were two of Vera's greatest
charms; "who would have thought that she had
ever been beaten by that brute Stanger, or had

sung in a provincial melodrama?" Of course he could not understand that these very incidents of her early life had helped to make her what she was. " I suppose it is her mixed blood that gives her that curious fascination of manner; she ought to be a trifle more stolid, however, with her undeniably Teutonic fair hair and complexion. But there is a suggestion of Southern blood in the tinting of her eyes and brows. Doubtless other people feel the fascination ! And I never asked her a single business question after all ! Is it possible that she did not *want* me to ask questions and kept me from remembering them by—— Pooh ! she was natural enough ! thoroughly unconscious of herself."

In which opinion Gaston Ravenscroft was mistaken. Vera was neither "natural" nor " unconscious" in his sense of the word. Her profession, as well as the reticences of her early life, had forced upon her an unusual amount of self-control, and, except in moments of strong excitement, she kept perpetual watch and ward over her words and actions. This self-control was caused by the natural recoil of a proud nature upon itself : the shame and distress that followed any

self-betrayal taught her to retreat into a shell of
reserve and apparent coldness at the faintest
token of dislike or indifference. The life of a
singer had its peculiar pains as well as pleasures
for her: she could throw herself heart and soul
into her public performances, but she suffered
agonies of painful reaction when they were over.
To avoid any display of this sensitiveness she
had taken refuge, as sensitive people often do,
in an exterior of impassive quietude. Only,
while with many people this impassiveness, this
quietude, is cold and disagreeable, with Vera it
assumed a peculiarly gentle and winning form,
and was more like humility than pride.

Ravenscroft found his way to her house on
the following afternoon, giving as excuse for his
reappearance the fact that he had not " talked
business " with her during the first interview.
He found her somewhat changed in manner.
They had parted on the friendliest terms; but
now she seemed to wish to set up a barrier.
There was almost a look of trouble in her eyes;
she gave him the wistful glance of a child who
longs, but is half afraid, to ask a question, and at
times she replied almost at random to his obser-

vations. He wondered slightly what was amiss, but concluded that some woman's whim that did not signify was at work within her, and that she would " come round " in time. So he simply disregarded her coldness and abstraction, and, after a formal request that he might ask a few questions about the present state of her affairs, he proceeded to put her through a keen catechism respecting her business arrangements, and her prospects for the future.

He could not find fault with the way in which she had been treated. It would have been rather a satisfaction to him to be able to demonstrate that he could have managed her affairs better than she and her friends had already managed them; but this satisfaction was denied him. He took upon himself unhesitatingly the part of censor, adviser, and guide; and although Vera might be surprised, and even a little amused by this tone, not knowing that he had a reason for it in his relationship to her, she was willing to allow him to retain it. She was even thankful to find a strong, staunch friend at her side.

Mrs. Cradock did not think it necessary to chaperon her young companion during Mr.

Ravenscroft's visits ; she looked upon him as Vera's guardian still, and was pleased to think that the girl had so efficient an adviser. Hence it came about that at four o'clock that afternoon, Vera and Mr. Ravenscroft found themselves alone in the pretty little drawing-room, with a good many papers between them and a sense of having discussed, if not transacted, a great deal of business.

"I hope you will acknowledge that even if I am not wise, my friends have been wise for me," Vera had said when the last paper had been inspected and silently returned to her.

"Ah, these same friends!" said Mr. Ravenscroft. "Who may they have been, Vera? You told me that you had made a good many: most of them in Germany, I suppose?"

"Yes, chiefly. I had Mrs. Cradock in England, but of course I made far more acquaintances at Rosenthal than I had done at Mrs. Cradock's school."

"Who were they?"

Vera considered. "There was the old organist, Kriegsthurm," she said, "and Dr. Müller, and Herr Krach, and Professor Weiss

—oh, almost all the professors were kind to me. Then Luise von Auersperg was my great school friend : her mother asked me once to spend a week at her house ; I was very happy there."

" A large family, I suppose."

" Yes, five sons and three daughters."

" Grown up ? "

" Luise was the fourth ; she was just my age."

Ravenscroft mused a little, seemed discontented, and presently asked, " Do you correspond with them ? "

" With Luise ? yes."

" And with none of her seven sisters and brothers ? "

There was some eagerness in his tone. Vera answered " No," with a look of such surprise that he felt ashamed of his question.

" And your professors ? Not interesting men, I imagine : snuffy old musicians with unkempt hair and long pipes, raving of their beloved art and nothing else—eh ? "

" Indeed," said Vera with spirit, " you are quite mistaken, Mr. Ravenscroft. They are very pleasant cultivated men, and advanced age was not a necessary qualification for a professorship. See — here is the photograph of Herr Krach ; what do you think of it ? ”

She moved a stand of photographs towards him and pointed to one of a decidedly handsome young man with dreamy dark eyes and long hair.

“ Is *he* a professor ? ”

“ Yes : a violinist.   A great friend of mine.”

“ Were all your professors after this fashion?”

“ No,” said Vera, smiling with genuine amusement, “ they were not so good-looking.”

“ But they all made much of you ? ”

“ They were very kind,” said Vera serenely.

Gaston threw himself back in his chair and looked savagely ill-humoured. Mademoiselle Vera gave him one considerate glance through her long eyelashes, and then confined her attention to the rings upon her fingers.

“ You have left them behind now, at any rate,” said Ravenscroft at last, with some complacency.   “ Well, you were probably right in coming away : you had been there long enough. That part of your life is done with.”

"Oh no; I have not done with it. I am going back to Germany in a year or two to visit my friends."

"In a year or two!—You will have formed plenty of other ties before then. I daresay you have met with friends in England already?"

"Yes, a few. Of course I have been obliged to make a good many acquaintances; but, I am almost afraid that I like Germans better than English people."

"Is the young man who brought me your note the other night a German?" said Ravenscroft, with what seemed to Vera striking irrelevance.

"No, he is not," she said slowly. Then the colour rose up into her fair face as she saw that Ravenscroft was scanning it with unusual attention. "He is a Russian."

"Indeed. Is *he* a friend of yours?"

In spite of herself Vera's cheeks retained their crimson hue, and her eyes began to look afraid. She answered very quietly, however. "Yes; I think he is."

It seemed as if Gaston Ravenscroft had not been altogether prepared for this reply. He continued his scrutiny of her blushing face for several minutes, with darkened brow and compressed lips; then he changed his position and asked another question—this time in a much lower voice.

"What position in life does your 'friend' fill?"

"He is a musician," said Vera.

"You met him—professionally, I suppose?"

She thought of the first interview in the street, and hesitated. "Yes," she said rather reluctantly; "I met him—first—on business."

"And *not* on business afterwards?"

"Exactly." She was recovering her self-possession.

Gaston opened his lips to say something hasty, then controlled himself and spoke in a gentle, conciliatory tone.

"My dear Vera, you are pleased to answer me as if there were some mystery concerning this young fellow. If there is any——"

"Oh, there is none," she answered proudly. "I had never spoken to him until he asked me to go with him to see poor Davy. You remember poor Davy, my old friend? He was ill, and sent me a message; that was how I began to know Mr. Guyon."

"Guyon? Is that his name?" Then Ravenscroft reflected awhile. "Does he play at concerts with you?"

"No."

"Where does he play then? I don't remember to have heard his name."

"He plays in the orchestra—at the Parthenon."

"Oh ho!"—Another long pause. "Can he do no more than that? He cannot be much of a performer, I suppose. Why does he not adopt some more lucrative profession?"

Vera was too angry to reply.

"A good-looking fellow too," said Mr. Ravenscroft magnanimously. "Something of a military turn about him; make a nice *jeune premier* on the stage, a capital 'walking gentleman.' Why do you not give him a helping hand, Vera?"

"He would not have accepted my help," said Vera in rather an ill-assured tone, "if I had offered it to him."

"What, you thought of offering it, then?" said Ravenscroft with a sudden start and glance towards her, while Vera remained dumb with astonishment at his quickness. He rose up and took a little turn about the room, as if not knowing what to say next. Finally he came and stood before her.

"I met this young man yesterday afternoon coming out of this house. He had been calling upon you, I suppose?"

"On business."

"Exactly. I have no wish to advance any claim of my own over you, Vera, but I do wish—I should like to think—that you would let *me* do your business for you."

"Musical business?" said Vera with a faint lifting of her delicate dark eyebrows.

"Did he come on musical business?" Ravenscroft asked dryly.

She looked up at him with her calm serious eyes, and said "No." But immediately afterwards a rush of colour dyed her forehead, cheeks, and throat to a burning crimson. She hung her head to conceal it, but the blush was only too evident to Gaston's keen eyes, and gave him a quick sharp pang. He was too much taken aback to be angry, and remained—rather unkindly, Vera thought—looking down upon her, knitting his eyebrows and pulling his moustache after his wont, and wondering why on earth women were such fools, and why Mrs. Cradock did not take better care of her charge. It was to her that he resolved to speak: he felt that there would be a want of delicacy in openly warning Vera that her conduct was liable to misconstruction.

But he had not reckoned upon Vera's acuteness or upon her courage. She suddenly looked up at him with her clearest, most open expression, and went straight to the heart of the subject.

"I know exactly what you think," she said. "You think that I am not acting as—as you would like your niece, Miss Ravenscroft, to act. You think I am, to say the least, ill-bred and unconventional. So I am. But you forget that I am merely a public singer—not a lady in your sense of the word. Oh, please don't interrupt me, for I know what I am saying. If a singer has not all the social privileges of a member of your class, she has at least some immunities."

"She has no immunity from scandal," muttered Gaston almost below his breath.

"She is a public character; she sees many people, talks to many people, whom she would never meet if she lived, as your niece lives, in a quiet country place, shielded from harm and responsibility in every way——"

"What do you know of my niece?"

"I saw her—twelve years ago." Vera was silent for a moment; he thought the tears rose to her eyes; but she went on steadily. "A singer is not bound by the rules that bind *her* youth and *her* inexperience. Do you think I have no visitors, Mr. Ravenscroft? Do you think I lead a nun's life? I have acquaintances of all kinds —chiefly among men: I meet them often and know them well——"

"Good heavens, Vera, and you told me you had so few friends!"

"Few *friends*, Mr. Ravenscroft, many acquaintances. Not many are allowed to enter this house: the few that come are here by special invitation."

"And you invited this fellow—this Guyon?"

"I am coming to that. Mr. Guyon has been asked to visit me if he hears anything concerning a matter in which he and I both are interested. My old friend, David Rowe, left us a certain trust, which we are anxious to carry out."

"A very unbecoming proceeding," said Ravenscroft coldly. "Of course a man of that kind knew no better than to place you in a position in which you would constantly be associated with this young fellow; but you might have refused to act. Come, Vera, give me the power to act in your place: tell me what the fiddler wanted doing and I will see this Mr. Guyon about it. You need not then have more to do with him at your house."

Vera turned away. "I have told you already," she said, "that he is my friend."

"If you have no one else to say it to you," Gaston replied, "I must take the privilege of an old acquaintance and tell you that the world will never believe in a mere friendship between a young man and a singer. The world will say that at least he is your—admirer." He had thought of a stronger term, but substituted this mild one in its stead.

"I hate the world!" said Vera impetuously. "What right has the world to interpose its odious suspicions—what right have *you*"—suddenly facing round upon him—"to suggest its suspicions to my mind ? You think you have a right to wound me, but you have none to insult me."

"Don't excite yourself, my dear Vera," said Ravenscroft, coolly regarding her. "You must not lay yourself open to remark if you dislike it so much. Tell me your business with this man and I will see that he does not trouble you for the future."

She looked at him with a sort of terror. "*You!*" she said. "You are the last person—at least—I beg your pardon—this business can be transacted by no one but myself and Mr. Guyon."

She left the room abruptly as she spoke, and Gaston Ravenscroft thought that he had reason for grave dissatisfaction at this state of affairs.

His anger was not lessened by a remark that Herbert made to him that evening as they met at a club, where each of them had been renewing old acquaintanceships. "By the by," he said, "I have remembered where I saw that young man who brought you Mademoiselle Vera's letter the other night. You know I told you that I had seen him before. I never forget a face."

" Where," said Ravenscroft sharply.

" In a van with other prisoners bound for Siberia."

" Are you sure of it ? "

" Certain. He was fainting with illness and fatigue when I saw him, but it was the same face."

" Political offenders, I suppose. Just the thing to touch a woman's heart—patriotism and all that kind of humbug."

" Unfortunately," said Herbert dryly, and with a certain reserve of manner, " these were not political offenders. I inquired at the time, out of sheer curiosity. Nothing so respectable."

" What had *he* done ? " said Gaston.

" He ? I am not sure that I know. I rather think," said Herbert reflectively, " that Mademoiselle Vera's friend was pointed out to me as the worst criminal of the party. So it might be well to put her on her guard."

" She is not very likely to listen to me," said Ravenscroft in a bitter tone.

" I have it," said Herbert suddenly. " I remember now. He had been exiled for conspiracy and murder. Yes ; that's the man."

CHAPTER XV.

AT NETHERBY.

RAVENSCROFT left London on the day following his second interview with Vera, and betook himself to Lincolnshire in order to pay a short visit to his mother, whom he had not seen for several years.

The separation had not been grievous either to mother or son, although the Baroness was sometimes heard to murmur that it was difficult to know what to say when people asked after Mr. Gaston Ravenscroft. But she was not ill pleased to have the management of her son's estate, and there was an amount of material gain to be derived from his absence, which she did not by any means despise. Her only desire for his return was founded upon the fact that a visit from him was an attention which she thought that

he ought to show. Ravenscroft himself was by
no means so devoted to his mother as to make
a long separation from her at all painful.

He arrived at Netherby late in the afternoon.
The day had been warm and bright; he sent on
his luggage by the carriage that had been ordered
to meet him, and resolved to walk to his mother's
house. His path lay across some broad green
meadows, then through a shady lane which would
bring him close to the village; then, as he well
knew, to the churchyard, which was used as a
public thoroughfare and opened upon a planta-
tion leading into Madame Waldstein's garden.
Had he a motive for choosing this pathway on
the day that brought him home after so many
years of absence?

He noted the different changes which years
had made in the buildings and the scenery
through which he passed; but his thoughts were
for the most part elsewhere—not with the friends
whom he was going to see, not with the dead
who lay beneath the churchyard soil, but with
a fair-faced girl whose voice and eyes were
perilously sweet, and whose greatest charm to
Gaston Ravenscroft lay in the fact that he felt

her to be as yet an enigma—a riddle that he knew not how to read.

He had crossed the fields and reached the stile which led to the shady lane. And here for a moment he paused as if he saw something that astonished and rather amused him. And yet there was nothing to be seen—except two young and handsome figures who were standing under the shade of an elm-tree, apparently in a very affectionate attitude. The girl's face was turned towards Mr. Ravenscroft, who recognised it at once as that of his niece Olivia. A very handsome face it was, with its well-cut features, bright complexion of the brunette order, and raven-black hair and eyes. He had seen more than one photograph of her, but he might have known her even without that aid, from the extraordinary likeness that she bore to a portrait of his mother in her youth. Even the slight elegant figure was the exact reproduction of Madame Waldstein's in that portrait; the slope of the fine shoulders, the haughty carriage of the defiant little head, would alone have served to convince Gaston of her relationship to his mother and therefore to himself.

But who was the young man who was kneeling on one knee before her with his head bent over the hand that he held in his own ? Gaston Ravenscroft was immediately conscious of a desire to attack the kneeling figure with his cane— an unreasonable desire which had to be carefully subdued before he could resolve to leap the stile and advance to disconcert the two young people.

For a moment he thought of passing them without apparent recognition, but in his present mood of idle and scornful indifference he could not resist the temptation of bringing into Olivia's pretty cheeks the scarlet flame of maiden modesty and making the unknown young man look ashamed of his indiscretion. So forward he went, with rather a cynical smile upon his lips.

To his surprise, however, neither of them moved a step. Miss Olivia still stood with her hand extended and her eyes cast down ; the young man bent his head over it with persevering assiduity. Mr. Ravenscroft was confounded, but more curious than ever.

" Thank you," he heard the girl's clear tones say as he approached ; " I think it's out now. Those thorns are most provoking."

" This was a very sharp fellow," said her companion, rising from his knee. " It has made your hand bleed, Olivia !"

But Olivia had turned from him impatiently, met Gaston's inquiring eyes, and sprung forward with a quick exclamation.

" It's Uncle Gaston ; I am sure it is !"

" I am equally sure that you are Olivia," said Mr. Ravenscroft, feeling relieved that the extraction of a thorn alone had been the delicate operation which required so reverential an attitude.

" Grandmamma was right," said the girl, who spoke in a rapid decisive way which her uncle was not sure that he liked, as she lifted her delicate face to be kissed. " She said you would come this way."

" Why ?"

" I do not know ; grandmamma is like a witch sometimes, and tells us things that we should never have thought of for ourselves. She told me to go by the churchyard and the lane, and I should meet you ; and behold, her words are true !"

Ravenscroft's brow darkened, but he made no

rejoinder, only turned a little towards the young man and seemed to wait for an introduction, which Olivia was not slow to give.

"This is a very old friend of mamma's, uncle," she said demurely. Gaston could not but smile at hearing this formal designation of the lad,—he did not seem to be more than nineteen,—and the young fellow himself reddened slightly as he heard it. He had a pleasant face, with a very winning expression, a complexion that changed colour like a girl's, lazy brown eyes, and dark brown hair. His forehead was good, his mouth sweet, but a little undecided; on close observation it could be seen that he had one or two tricks of manner, which a public school would have corrected—one, a habit of holding his head slightly on one side, and half shutting his eyes when he was considering a subject; another, a soft slow dainty way of speaking which caused him at times to be called affected. He was tall and slenderly built, but, although in the lanky stage, he moved with an ease and grace and spoke with a readiness which showed him to be more accustomed to the ways of the world than was at first quite apparent. In spite of the clear red of those uncomfortable blushes (quite as pretty in their way as any of Olivia's, and a greater embellishment to his dark face than he could have imagined), his manners were marked by an unembarrassed courtesy which was singularly little like the *mauvaise honte* of an English boy at eighteen, and proceeded, perhaps, from the fact that he had spent much of his life abroad. Mr. Ravenscroft felt an involuntary attraction to him, which, strange to say, was succeeded by an entirely different feeling as Olivia continued her introductory speech.

"Mamma asked him to come and take care of me," she said. "I daresay you know his name, uncle. Mr. Lancelot Aylmer."

Ravenscroft's face suddenly changed. It assumed its coldest and sternest expression as he slightly returned Mr. Lancelot Aylmer's courteous salutation. The chilliness of his demeanour struck both young people with surprise. Olivia drew up her head with some offence. Lancelot reddened—this time with visible annoyance, and said in his quiet dulcet tones,

"I will go home by the fields, if you will

excuse me, Olivia. I have to call somewhere in the village for Mr. Hervey."

" Oh, very well. We shall see you this evening."

" No, I think not, thanks. Good afternoon."

He lifted his hat and turned back. It seemed to Ravenscroft that she looked disappointed, but as she walked onwards with him she did not give any outward expression to this feeling in words. She only said,

" If Cousin Richard wants him, of course he must go. He is bound hand and foot to Cousin Richard. You remember them very well, do you not, Uncle Gaston ? "

" I remember Richard Hervey, of course."

" And Lance too."

" I have heard of him from my mother."

" Ah, of course he had scarcely come here when you were at home last," said Olivia, reflectively. " He is Cousin Richard's ward, you know. I always thought that guardians were obliged to educate their wards properly."

" Does Richard Hervey not educate this lad properly ? " said Gaston with a certain grimness of tone.

"Mamma and I do not think so," said Olivia, decidedly. "Lance wanted to decide on his profession a year or two ago; the army was what he would have preferred, but Cousin Richard would not allow him to go in for the examinations. Lance says sometimes that he will go and enlist as a private."

"A very suitable rank and profession."

Olivia detected the satire, but did not guess against whom it was levelled; she laughed, therefore, merrily, and continued:

"He thought Cousin Richard meant him to go to Oxford, perhaps, but he cannot tell; Cousin Richard says nothing decisive. Don't you think it is odd, Uncle Gaston?"

"I should advise you to leave your Cousin Richard Hervey and his affairs alone, Olivia. Depend upon it, if he has adopted this lad, or is bringing him up, he will doubtless do what best befits his future station in life."

Olivia arched her eyebrows and telegraphed signals of astonishment to the hedgerows.

"I thought that University training was suitable to any gentleman," she said in an undertone.

" Possibly."

"Then it is suitable for Lance?" She flashed an eager glance at him and seemed to expect a reply ; but he gave her none of a kind that satisfied her. He began questioning her concerning the building of some houses in the neighbourhood, and would not allow her to return to the subject of Mr. Hervey's treatment of his ward.

Once or twice, however, she nearly stopped in the middle of her gay chatter about the news of the place, for she saw that his eyes were absently fixed on the gray church tower, and that his thoughts were evidently far away. But if she paused he immediately inserted a question so very much to the point that she, baffled and disconcerted, was obliged to go on with the trivial recital.

They reached the house after a time, and Gaston underwent the salutations of his friends with resignation rather than with joyfulness. In fact, there was now and then to be perceived in his manner a touch of scornful impatience, especially when Madame Waldstein expressed any pleasure at the meeting. At these moments

Gaston's gesture and glance would give the impression that his thoughts ran in some such fashion as this : " Why do you say you are glad to see me ?　Would you not rather by far that I had left my bones to bleach on the steppes or in the desert than come here to claim the right that you have grudged me ever since Philip died ?" And then the reflection would follow : "Was it worth while to come back ?　Would it not be well to settle the bulk of the estate on Philip's daughter and go back to the East ? "　But he never entertained the proposition seriously for a moment.　There was one word which seemed to him sufficient as protest, reason, and refutation alike, and that one word was—*Vera*.　If no one else needed him, he was sure that Vera did.

The old Baroness looked frail, and was almost unable to move from her couch, or the chair to which she was carried in the afternoons ; but she was as magnificently dressed, her eye was as keen, and her tongue as sharp, as ever.　Having made a decent show of pleasure at her son's return she deemed it expedient to begin a course of searching questions respecting his reasons for it, but obtained very few satisfactory answers.

"You are reserved," she said to him at last, putting up her eye-glasses and glancing him over with the sort of delicate scorn which he had been accustomed to receive from her since the days of his infancy; "you say no more than you can help, apparently."

"Did I ever say more than I could help?" said her son indifferently, as he pinched the ears of a little Skye terrier that had climbed into his lap. He was lying back in an easy chair, long-limbed, muscular, and bronzed; he seemed almost out of place in Madame Waldstein's small and dainty chamber. The Baroness looked at him fixedly, noting every distinctive point, good or bad, about him—the strong frame, the dark, proud head, the dauntless eyes and stormy brow, the haughty lip and the rapidly changing expression of his features, in which fire and gloom seemed alternately to predominate, and then said quietly,

"You have grown rather like your father."

"Is that intended for a compliment?"

"That is an uncivil return for it, if it were. However, you never piqued yourself on your civility to me; you expended it in other directions, I believe."

“Not entirely, I hope,” said Gaston, restoring to her a handkerchief which she had dropped, with a little bow and ironical smile; “I keep some for home consumption.”

Then he relapsed into careless silence, and looked out upon the lawn, where Mrs. Ravenscroft and her daughter were walking together. Olivia had slipped her hand through her mother’s arm; Felicia’s graceful head was bent a little, as if to listen to the girl’s confidences. The day was closing, and a soft stillness had fallen over all the scene. The Baroness averted her eyes from Gaston’s face, and looked at the couple in the garden.

“Well, what do you think of Philip’s daughter?” she said suddenly and sharply. “She is a pretty child, is she not?”

“I cannot compliment her more than by saying that she is very like the portrait of yourself, taken just after your marriage, Madame,” said Gaston.

“Prettier,” said the Baroness; “but not so attractive.”

“That would be impossible—doubtless.”

“My dear Gaston, satire is a formidable

weapon when well used ; but it is not very powerful in your hands.   I suppose you did not need
it among the Asiatics ?"

"No," said her son, with imperturbable composure ; "a revolver would have gone further."

"And accordingly it has grown a little rusty.
I will tell you, if you will do me the favour to
listen, what Olivia wants : it is polish and experience. She is as clever as she can be; but
her mother has done her best to mew her up in
this country village and blunt the child's wits as
much as possible."

"I thought she seemed bright enough. She
has a great opinion of the blessings of education."

"Education ! Oh yes," said Madame Waldstein scornfully ; "she is a little blue-stocking in
her way. You know Felicia was always something of the *femme savante;* she was brought up
on all the sciences ; and poor dear Philip encouraged her and thought that she would prove
a second De Staël or Récamier. I could have
told him better. Felicia never had a grain of
savoir faire; she could not have been a great
lady to save her life."

"Felicia seems to me exceedingly graceful and dignified."

"Possibly; but you have been out of the world for ten years, Gaston. Felicia is old-fashioned and has old-fashioned notions, which I am very much afraid that Olivia has imbibed. She is a girl that ought to make a good marriage —I might say a great one. She is a beauty, and she has social gifts: she must have a career."

"Certainly, let her have one by all means."

"I am glad you see it in that light," said Madame Waldstein, with a bird-like turn of her small head, and a covert smile; "for the matter is in your hands."

"Mine?"

"I suppose you know that you are the head of the family?" said the Baroness, beginning to wave her fan up and down before her face. "Or perhaps your residence abroad has led you to forget a fact of which we are—painfully— aware."

For the first time Gaston winced a little, and his mother was aware that he did so. It was in his curtest manner that he replied:

"It would be more to the point if you told me

what, as head of the family, you expected me to do.”

“Really, Gaston, you are too much of a lout,” said the Baroness, with a laugh of the finest scorn. “It is positively repellent to my feelings to discuss any matter with you.”

“Because I refuse to beat about the bush? Because I prefer frankness and openness to deceit?”

“There is no deceit in the matter. You are violent, Gaston,” said his mother composedly. “Remember that you are in a civilised country.”

The man’s eyes glowed like coals of fire, but he spoke in determinedly low tones. “I may be violent,” he said; “but I will not be false. I come from the tribe of Ishmael, where I found a companionship that suited me; for surely, like Ishmael himself, I had found that my hand was against every man’s, and every man’s hand against me. But whose fault was that?”

“Your own,” said Madame Waldstein, striking a table beside her a smart blow with the closed sticks of her fan—“your own, and no one’s beside.” And she struck the table again, as if she wished the table had been her son.

“ I think not,” said he firmly. “ It was early in my life when I found out the difference that you made between my brother and me—a difference that embittered the years of my boyhood. Then, when I came to later life, who was it that alienated my brother from me but yourself? Who was it that drove me to take a step which was as premature as it was rash, and which was as nearly my ruin as it could have been? You may not have done all this knowingly, but you did it; and I defy you to wonder at my long absence from home, or my coldness and violence, as you term it, on my return.”

Madame Waldstein’s eyes glittered like hard bright stones during this address. “ All that I did was entirely for the best,” she said haughtily. “ You have not recited all the benefits that I conferred upon you, however. I suppose your later remarks refer to your connection with my maid, Lucy Moore. It was owing to my proposition of informing your brother of that very disreputable love affair that you took her away from my service, and went with her to Elmstone.”

Gaston started and changed colour. “ To Elmstone ? ” he said. “ I did not know——”

"That I knew where you went? I knew all about you," said Madame Waldstein with complacency. "But I did not betray you to Philip, because I thought that you had sufficiently ruined your prospects without losing the allowance that he was kind enough to make you. I let the matter go on quietly."

Her son, resting his chin on his hands, glanced at her as if doubtful of her motives for this consideration.

"I knew that the affair would transpire sooner or later, and so I let it alone. But it went on longer than I anticipated. I grew impatient. It went on for four years, I believe. Part of the time was spent at Elmstone and part abroad."

She glanced at him furtively with a little smile, then looked away.

"Well?" said Gaston, with a mixture of impatience and anxiety. "Anything more? Poor Phil's death put an end to the secrecy—and I had had secrecy enough to last me all my life, God knows!—and then, after all, there was nothing to be told—nothing to be done. She died."

"Yes, she died," said the old lady, with that significant little smile which gave to her face something sinister and unpleasant, in spite of her delicate bloom, her snow-white hair, her handsome features and sparkling eyes. "She died—but she left you first."

The colour forsook her son's face. A look of fear and pain came into it. "Mother," he said huskily, "you do not mean—you cannot say that you—*you*—know more of the reasons for her departure than I do?"

"What should I know?" said the Baroness, with a mocking laugh. "Suppose I wanted to tease you—you are easily teased, you know, my dear Gaston—I might say that I had managed the whole business, that *I* had tracked you, watched you, deceived you, separated you—deceiving her as much as ever you thought she had deceived you——"

"If that were true," said Gaston, with a face of ashes, in which his eyes seemed to be the only live points, "if that were true, I never would forgive you."

His mother took a rapid survey of his face, then laughed aloud. "You are a fool, Gaston," she said contemptuously. "You were made to be deceived."

"Tell me whether it is true or not," he said, starting to his full height and towering over her with so threatening a brow that she shrank a little in spite of herself.

"*Not* true, of course," she said hastily. "I know nothing about her." But as he turned away she could not forbear sending after him a Parthian shot. "Even if it were true, I should be loath to tell you so," she said with a sort of scornful pity. "Not for my own sake—oh no! but for the suffering that I see I should inflict."

"What suffering can *you* inflict?" he asked harshly, although his set stern face gave the lie to his words. "It is twelve years since I lost her. I am hardened now."

"Ah yes," said Madame Waldstein dryly. "So I thought when I sent Olivia to meet you by way of Netherby Churchyard."

This was more than Ravenscroft could endure. He stood bolt upright for a moment, with his hand clenching itself at his side and the veins swelling upon his broad forehead, then turned and left the room without a word. The Baroness followed him with her eyes and laughed to herself significantly.

"It would be easy still to make him believe that she was false," she murmured to herself. "Is it worth while to do it? Hardly, perhaps. But he is such a fool—so easily tricked—that one is tempted to see how far matters could be carried! However, one must not try too many things at once. It seems never to occur to him to doubt our story about the boy's death; but I wish Richard Hervey would be more careful in avoiding suspicion. Who would have thought to see him so absurdly devoted to that lad as he has been for the last five years? If Gaston were not blind he would certainly guess the truth!"

CHAPTER XVI.

MADAME WALDSTEIN'S VIEWS.

BOTH Madame Waldstein and Gaston had said more than they had intended, and also left unsaid a great deal that they had meant to say. Gaston had been irritated to a point that, a few years earlier, would have impelled him to leave his mother's house as he had done upon that day of Vera Marlitt's unlucky visit; but he had gained in stubbornness, if not in self-control, since that time, and would not allow himself to yield to the promptings of his own ill-humour. He contented himself with avoiding another private colloquy with his mother, and succeeded for a day and a half; at the end of which time she sent him a peremptory message that she wished to speak to him in her own room. It was Olivia who brought the message, and she came in armed with a racquet, which had a most business-like appearance. Gaston had been out nearly all the previous day, and had scarcely seen her that morning.

“Where have you been all day?” he asked, as he rose, looking rather reluctant, Olivia thought, to leave the little library which had been turned for him into a smoking-room.

“I? Oh, I am always busy in a morning,” she said, as if surprised at the question. “This morning I was reading German with mamma from nine till ten, then I practised and painted until lunch.”

“Not out all day?”

“I have a tennis-match to play this afternoon, so I rested all the morning. Look, Uncle Gaston, I won this racquet last year. Do you see my name on the silver plate? I was the champion player of the neighbourhood!”

“Shall you win the prize this year too?”

“Oh, no. Lance is sure to win it. He has been practising this season. In fact he might have won it last year if he had chosen, for he can play splendidly when he likes; but he was too lazy. He is waking up this year.”

Gaston was silent, and watched the young beauty as she flitted about the room, altering the position of a chair here, a book there, and seeming to put things in order almost without knowing it. Her lissom figure was well displayed in a tennis costume of white flannel, embroidered with wild roses in coloured silks round the neck and wrists and skirt. Presently she turned round and laughed.

"Uncle Gaston, I don't wish to hurry you, but grandmamma is not accustomed to be kept waiting, and she was ready to see you when I left her. Ah, there's the pony-carriage. I wish you were coming with us, uncle. We are going to bring my dearest friend home with me—Ilma Zaranoff; she is going to stay a few days with us."

"Zaranoff? I know the name. Who is she?"

"She was the daughter of one of grandmamma's friends in Vienna. She married a Russian count; and she has lived a great deal in Paris. She is so beautiful, Uncle Gaston!"

"And the Russian count, where is he?"

"Oh, he died soon after the marriage. But

do go to grandmamma; she will say that I have never delivered her message if you don't make haste."

Ravenscroft went accordingly to his mother's room. He found Madame Waldstein lying upon an invalid couch, with a fretful, wearied look upon her face, which, as yet, had not undergone the "making-up" essential to her appearance in public, and was therefore startlingly sallow and wrinkled. She had many costly lace-trimmed wrappings about her, and the curtains were drawn so that the daylight should not shine fully upon her face and show the ravages that Time had made; yet enough could be seen to impress her son with the conviction that his mother was an older and feebler woman than he had thought, and to soften his tone and manner towards her in no slight degree.

She was talking to her maid when he entered, and also engaged in feeding a great white cat, which had its seat on a cushion at her side. To Gaston she vouchsafed, therefore, very little attention.

"I tell you, Alice, I will not have pink roses, and that is enough. Do you imagine that I wish to dress like Miss Ravenscroft ? Something rich and simple is what an old woman ought to wear. Mimi, my darling, will you not eat then ? My precious, it is cream, not milk ; do not turn away thy pretty little head. An aigrette, Alice, or the diamond clasp which I wear with my gray satin, or perhaps the beetles with ruby eyes—oh, what an imbecile you are ! Am I always to repeat that—— Mimi, my Mimi, you would not leave me ? "

" I understood, madame, that you wished to speak to me," said her son dryly. " If you are engaged, I will come at another time."

" Ah, Gaston, sit down," said his mother carelessly, as if she had but just perceived him. " Don't be impatient ; I shall be ready directly. If you had come when I sent for you—Alice, for heaven's sake, do not put yellow and pink together. And see, you have let Mimi upset her saucer. Was ever anybody surrounded by such a set of idiots as I am ? And there is Mimi going ! My angel ! my Mimi——"

" And I also," said Gaston. " My dear mother, I will come back when you are able to converse with me."

"You will do nothing of the kind," said the Baroness peremptorily, dropping her querulous tone at once. "Go away, Alice. Take the saucer with you, and let Mimi out. What are you crying about, little fool? Pick up the ribbons and go."

Alice, a pretty trim little damsel, whose eyes were now dim with tears, groped rather feebly after her belongings; and Gaston, half compassionate, half impatient, stooped to assist her. She curtsied in a frightened way, and made her exit with speed; after which, Mr. Ravenscroft shut the door after her, and returned to his mother's side to find her watching him with half shut eyes.

"Don't interfere with my maids any more, Gaston," said the terrible old woman with a curl of malicious pleasure about her lips. "You did that once too often. Lucy was the best servant I ever had before you came across her."

"You will put me under the necessity of leaving your house altogether if you allude to that subject again," said Gaston, with a sudden light in his gloomy eyes. "I must request you not to mention *her* name for the future."

"Not a pleasant subject, is it?" said the Baroness, charmed at being able to wound him so easily, but with an air of spurious sympathy. "I do not wonder that you avoid it, poor Gaston." Then, as a gesture told her that she was going too far, she added hastily: "However it was not of *that* that I wished to speak: it was about Olivia. We strayed from the point a little the other day. Will you not sit down, Gaston?"

"Thanks, no, I prefer to stand. It is about Olivia that I also wish to speak."

"How curious! Well, dear Gaston, suppose you say what you have to say first, then I will tell you my little projects."

"As you please. I thought of speaking to Felicia, but feared that she might be distressed by my question. Is it her wish, or yours, that Olivia should be so absurdly intimate with that boy of Richard Hervey's?"

"Lancelot Aylmer? Richard's ward?" said the Baroness, looking at him steadily, with completely arrested attention, and some little curiosity.

"Richard Hervey's son, whom he does not choose to acknowledge," said Ravenscroft shortly.

Madame Waldstein continued to gaze at him
for several seconds with an inscrutable expression which might have been astonishment, perplexity, or even amusement, and which Gaston
found decidedly vexatious. Presently, however,
she averted her eyes, took up her fan and began
to examine its feathery tips, while she said in a
tone of almost exaggerated interest :

"Is that really true ? How very romantic!
How did you hear of it, Gaston ? I suppose
Cousin Richard Hervey did not tell you ?"

"I heard it years ago from Marshall," said
her son, mentioning his solicitor's name. "Of
course I am not certain that the report is true ;
but if not, I should like to know who the fellow
is, and where he comes from. He and Olivia
seem to be like brother and sister."

"Indeed they do," said Madame Waldstein,
sighing. "Really, I wish we had heard this story
sooner. A most unfortunate complication!——"

It seemed to Gaston that she was half smiling
as she said the words. He turned upon her
angrily. "You do not want her to marry him,
I suppose. Is this the great marriage that you
planned for your granddaughter ?"

" Do not speak so loudly, Gaston ; you make my head ache. Marry him ! poor dear Olivia knows better than to dream of such a thing. Besides they are both children, and he is only Olivia's age. They have played together— that is all."

" And why did they ever play together ? It is a most unsuitable acquaintance. How is it that you are so friendly with your cousin now, mother ? You were on very different terms in the old days."

Madame Waldstein spread out her hands with a gesture of repudiation. " I friendly with Richard Hervey ! I detest the man. He is useful to me sometimes, that is all. It is Felicia you may blame, not me. She pities him, pities the boy, pities everybody. I cannot control Felicia's pitiful tendencies. Take care that you do not have Hervey for a brother-in-law, Gaston. I am continually expecting that announcement. With a cousin it is always possible."

" She could not care for Richard Hervey."

" She never cared for Philip, yet she married him. You talk like a schoolgirl, Gaston, instead of a man of eight-and-thirty. Well, now that you know the dangers that beset your path, will you take my advice and get those two women to London, or somewhere?   Olivia ought to be presented."

"I have been too long out of England to be able to manage such matters."

"A mere excuse, Gaston.   All that I want you to do is to tell Felicia what her duty is with respect to Olivia.   It will come with more effect from you than from me.   I am tired of talking. If they decide on going, Lady Wylde will present Felicia.   I believe she is going up to town in two or three weeks' time with Ilma Zaranoff."

" Ah, by the by, who is she?"

"Ilma Zaranoff?   Her mother was Natalie von Löwenstein, one of my dearest friends when I was in Vienna.   She died of a fever when Ilma was two or three years old—a lovely little thing the child was then : I was her godmother—and her husband, Josef von Löwenstein died soon afterwards, leaving the daughter in the care of his friend, old Count Zaranoff."

" I see—her future husband," said Gaston carelessly.

"Not at all : listen.   He and his wife took

care of the little one, and in course of time betrothed her to their son, Count Maurice—such a handsome boy !—but very wild and eccentric in his ways. He was first a page, then he entered the guards, and we all thought that the marriage would take place immediately, when every one who knew them was electrified by the news that he had mixed himself up in some Revolutionary intrigues, particularly with a set of Polish fanatics called Strolenski. Don't you know the name, Gaston ?"

" Not at all. Pray go on : I am very much interested."

" Countess Zaranoff belonged to a Polish family herself : I suppose that the son inherited some of her opinions. He—Count Maurice—concealed the Strolenskis in his own house, and actually fired on the officers who came to arrest them! I believe that he killed one of them! At any rate, he was also arrested and exiled to Siberia."

" And she ?—" Gaston's face expressed some curiosity ; " she—married him and accompanied him, I suppose ?"

Madame Waldstein shrugged her shoulders.

“My dear Gaston, you are — inconceivable!” she said.

“Oh . . . Then the old Countess was dead and she married the father instead?”

“Pray allow me to finish my story; I have a good reason for telling it to you. The parents were both dead by this time, and Maurice Zaranoff had inherited the estates. These estates were forfeited. Of course you could not expect Ilma von Löwenstein to sacrifice all her prospects and marry a man in that position! The engagement was broken; and she married shortly afterwards a distant—very distant—cousin of Maurice Zaranoff’s; and upon the marriage the Emperor settled upon them all Maurice Zaranoff’s estates, and made the cousin take the title of Count. So Ilma became Countess Zaranoff in spite of Maurice’s banishment.”

“Rather hard upon the exiled Zaranoff,” said Gaston, musing a little as his mother paused. “What became of him?”

“Of him! I suppose that he is still working in the mines at Siberia,” said the Baroness loftily. “A happy release for Ilma.”

“Was he so depraved?”

"He must have been odious to join those abominable Nihilists. I think that he was a little mad. She would have suffered tortures had she married him. He was spending his whole income on the Revolutionary party."

"Vile wretch!" said Gaston satirically. Then with a keen glance and a bending of his brows, he asked, "You have no reason to think that he has escaped from Siberia?"

"Not in the least. What makes you think so?"

"Oh, nothing. And—excuse me—but considering that you have spent the last fifteen years in England, you seem remarkably well acquainted with the family history of these Zaranoffs. Were they friends of yours?"

"Yes, all of them. But I hear the news of the world from various sources, although I am a prisoner in Netherby! The Longmores correspond with me still; they told me the history of Count Maurice and Ilma von Löwenstein. Ilma has been staying with them in London."

"Who are the Longmores?"

"My dear Gaston! You *must* remember

Sir Adrian Longmore—the old General! He used to stay here in your father's time."

"Yes; I remember him."

"He was a great friend of the Zaranoffs—a connection by marriage, I believe—guardian to the young Count until he attained his majority. Maurice Zaranoff used to spend half his time with the Longmores when they were living at Vienna and afterwards in London. If you had been in town you would certainly have met him."

"Ah, yes," said Gaston, who was becoming weary of the subject, and certainly did not attend as closely to the last few sentences as he might have done. "Ah, yes; but may I ask, mother, why you take the trouble to relate to me this interesting story?"

Madame Waldstein looked him full in the face and played with her fan. "Can you not guess?" she said.

Gaston shook his head.

"Ilma Zaranoff is a widow. She has a large property; she is young and beautiful. I know of no person whom I would sooner receive as a daughter-in-law," said the Baroness.

"I see. But I do not intend to marry again." said Gaston coldly. "And if I did, I would not take a woman who had broken off her engagement to a man merely because he was poor and in disgrace."

"Bah! that is your romantic side. I thought we had had enough of that in old days. Your travels in Asia have left you with as little knowledge of the world as ever."

Her son made no answer. He pulled his moustache and looked blankly out of the window.

"Madame Zaranoff is coming here to-day," continued the Baroness in a dryly suggestive tone. "I shall be glad of her society and advice for Olivia. I shall be obliged to you, Gaston, at any rate, if you will pay her a certain amount of attention. She is a person worth cultivating, for she goes everywhere, and is greatly esteemed. I think it is a compliment to Olivia that Ilma has taken such a fancy to her."

Gaston shrugged his shoulders and was silent. The old lady, looking into his dark and dissatisfied countenance, and feeling that he had been worsted at more points than one, was seized with a fleeting curiosity to know the real reason of his return to England.   She asked a question sharply.

"What brought you home, Gaston?"

"Anxiety to see my relations."

"That is so likely!   What beside?"

"No other reason.   There was one relation of mine, at least, whom I came to see."

"And that was——"

"Hervey's granddaughter, Vera."

"Oh, that girl!   I remember her; a little wizened wretch who shocked Felicia by singing a vulgar comic song when you brought her here."

"She is now a beautiful woman and a fine singer."

"Indeed?   And you came home to see *her?*"

"I regret that I did not do so earlier," said Gaston composedly.   "I had forgotten how long it was since she came here, and fancied her only seventeen or eighteen.   She is now nearly three-and-twenty, I believe.   Yes, I came back to see her, and to persuade Richard Hervey, if possible, to do something for her."

"Do you think you can persuade Richard Hervey to do anything?"

"I shall try."

" You have great faith in yourself," said Madame Waldstein ironically.

" I have faith in my cause. Have you anything else to say to me, mother? If not, I will ask you to excuse me. I have a good deal of business to transact."

He took his departure, glad to get away without a quarrel, and Madame Waldstein was left to her own reflections, which were not of an unpleasing kind.

The old intriguer thought that she had managed her work very well. She was delighted to find that Gaston believed Lancelot Aylmer to be Mr. Hervey's son, for it was she herself who had caused a story to this effect to be conveyed to Gaston's ears. Ever since Mr. Hervey had insisted upon bringing the boy home from a French school, where he had been placed for a certain length of time, Madame Waldstein had been devising plausible stories to account in Gaston's eyes for his presence at Netherby. The supposed relationship between Lancelot— or rather Bertram Ravenscroft—and Mr. Hervey, was a very happy flight of her imagination, especially as she could see that Gaston was

developing a strong prejudice against the lad.
If the Baroness could have had her own way, she
would not have allowed the boy to come within
a hundred miles of Netherby; but Mr. Hervey
had taken the matter into his own hands and
declared that Lancelot (as they called him) should
be as a son to him, and should live with him at
Netherby Manor. Madame Waldstein was terribly afraid lest Gaston should learn the truth
during his visit; but she hoped that it would
not be a long one, and she did not intend to
make it particularly pleasant. A few more
scenes such as she already had with him, and she
knew that he would leave the house in a rage,
and perhaps return to it no more.

She did not want him to marry, and she
believed that her suggestion respecting Countess
Zaranoff's fitness for him as a wife would
decidedly prejudice him against that young lady.
The old Baroness knew her son's weaknesses of
temper exceedingly well. She was trying all
means to induce him to leave Netherby, even
while she seemed most anxious for him to stay.

The incipient love-affair between Olivia and
Lancelot must also be crushed before it went

any further. If Gaston were to take Felicia and Olivia to London and remain there with them until he left England for the East once more, Madame Waldstein thought that she could sleep in peace. She had set her heart upon Olivia's becoming the heiress of Ravenscroft.

END OF VOL. I.

Printed by R. & R. CLARK, *Edinburgh.*

G. C. & Co.